Drowning in Darkness

Peter Oliva

Drowning in Darkness

Cormorant Books

Second Printing, January, 1994.

Published with the assistance of the Canada Council, the Ontario Arts Council, the Government of Ontario through the Ministry of Culture and Communications, and Multiculturalism and Citizenship Canada.

Cover image from an original (lithograph, serigraph and relief) print entitled *Pioneers: The Context* by Julie McIntyre, courtesy of the artist.

Cover design by Artcetera Graphics, Dunvegan, Ontario.

Edited by Gena K. Gorrell.

Published by   Cormorant Books Inc.,
                      RR 1, Dunvegan, Ontario K0C 1J0.

Printed and bound in Canada.

Canadian Cataloguing in Publication Data

Oliva, Peter,1964-
    Drowning in darkness

ISBN 0-920953-51-4

        I. Title.

PS8579.L325D76 1993   C813'.54   C93-090331-5
PR9199.3.O54D76 1993

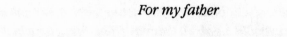

For my father

I have spoken of Coghlan and his acting elsewhere, but a curious fact was told me about the end of that fine actor which I must set down. After the run of Romeo and Juliet, he was engaged to play in a piece at the Shaftesbury Theatre which was not a success. He returned to America and never came back to England again. In about a year, I think, he died at Galveston. Shortly after his burial there a great storm came up from the Gulf which swept his coffin with others into the sea. The Gulf Stream bore him round Florida, up the coast about fifteen hundred miles to Prince Edward Island, and he came ashore not far from his home.

    —Sir Johnston Forbes-Robertson,
      A Player under Three Reigns

The sea that washes the Sicilian shore swelled up, and became, for ten miles in length, like a chain of dark mountains; while the waters near our Calabrian coast grew quite smooth, and in an instant appeared as one clear polished mirror. . . .

    —Father Angelucci, 15 August 1643,
      H. Swinburne's *Travels in the Two Sicilies*

ONE

What she sees:

There is darkness inside a mountain that is unlike the night, another world where methane swirls next to the coal face like a warm current in black sea. The gas seeps through mine-shafts and tunnels, marbling both rock and air. It seduces a miner to sleep, to dream, to abandon life. An invisible river quietly winds past his cheek, under his nose, threatening to carry him away. One breath and all his senses leave him, or perhaps he leaves them. His brain numbs, frozen on his last thought. His legs buckle, suddenly boneless. And then he dreams.

The gas softens the cobbles, eggs, nuts, peas and fines of coal into sponge, cushioning the miner's fall. It penetrates and turns coal soft, making the rock just as boneless as his legs. But more often than not the methane pulls him further away than the coal floor, further into darkness. Carried along by sleep, with the current tugging, swirling around him, he drifts deeper into the mountain. Hours later, his safety light fades in the distance.

Older, more experienced miners tame the gas and channel it to dig their coal for them. By redirecting the fresh air coming up through the man-way with huge tarred curtains they steer those same swirls of methane toward the face. They work the gas back into the face, expanding the coal, bubbling soft coal chunks right out of the wall, scraping away layers of darkness. Coal sponges tumble from the seam, along with iron deposits the size of skulls that threaten to break bones and crack heads. The methane rivers probe the face and the coal bounces, gets shovelled back, dropped down, railed out.

Horses, as slow and smudged as chinook-filled skies, haul the coal cars up through the tunnel and out toward daylight.

As the miners move further into the seam, minute shards of dust hang in the air, wash over their leather boots and eventually flood the tunnel with more than just darkness and gas. The men twist and swim through this dust. The coal peppers through them and they push themselves through shadows that move only grudgingly.

There is Celi: carving the darkness, breathing Turtle Mountain's dust, breathing the mountain itself and carrying its dust out of the mine with black, portmanteau lungs. Celi: with coal cheesed under his nails. Celi: wet and grainy, dust spreading like sepia over his body, making his hair thick and blue-black, his skin shoe-shined into darkness. Celi: finally becoming the mountain, the water, coal seams, rock shards and all. Disappearing.

He cannot see anything except what his head-lamp lights for him. Water, almost invisible to the pinprick of light in front of him, dribbles down the walls, veining his night. The brattice curtain bulges beside him, holding back the clean air, while gas flutters against the coal face.

And through this fog, through currents of methane, dust and stone, Celi steers the curtain like a sail, one hand on the tarp's mast, the other on his pick, clearing rooms with clean, straight lines. As he moves further into what was once, only a moment ago, solid black rock, he bends the currents, sparing coal pillars that sustain his tunnel. The men behind him support these pillars with ten-foot timbers that grow and stretch thin within minutes to meet the cap rock. The ground is rising. The floor heaves under their feet, defies gravity every second. Timbers pivot and creak into place, groaning to each other as they hold down the floor, as they push up the roof. Foot by foot the men hammer and wedge their timbers into frames and cross-sections, following Celi into the seam as if escaping a wooden skeleton that forever chases them.

With invisible breakers of methane and dust billowing in front of him, Celi sails his men away, through the mountain's moonless darkness.

*

Maybe he never knew her at all.

Maybe Pep lived with her for eleven-odd years, treading back and forth between the same family portraits, treading just as redolently between the same dream-worn blankets and the same time-worn memories, like a sleep-walker, and never really knew her, never really saw her.

After Sera left, any whisper of her name brought the same response: the faintest shadow of doubt would inch across his face like a thin pool stretching for a deeper, darker place. The shadow disappeared, slowly, under an ear, at his whisker's curb. And after that there would be a moment of silence, a move toward his finger of scotch, then a slight shrug of his shoulders. Nothing more.

The end.

And nothing would have changed, nothing except, in a small way, some sort of fleeting vindication for Sera: all in the time it took to blow out a candle. But not even the puff of a spoken word was needed to do that much. He didn't say anything. His face left, then returned, after its brief escape, to where he'd left it; her story walled up as though she had never existed.

She's not here, he could have said. What does it matter?

Sometimes he shrugged the same way when he was completely alone, or sitting at a terrycloth bar table, mid-afternoon, and at those times he was just one old man among many who sipped their beer, leaned back in their chairs and either winced, nodded or smiled at where life had left them.

Pep winced. And then he shrugged.

Most people were surprised he was still alive, sagging almost everywhere, but still alive. But their memory of him was sagging too, so that when they saw him they propped their recollections up with imaginary poles, and planted those images beside the little man—squinting as he came out of the bar, his clothes loose, dragging, his hat sweat-stained and thumb-polished—and they saw several Peps, each identical to the others. That may have been the surprise: their tattered memories of the man were exactly who he had aged into. No guessing, no wondering: that was Pep, Pep Rogolino, exactly as they would have imagined him.

Whatever secrets he kept stayed lodged, unmined and buried in his pores—even the secrets he kept from himself. Those secrets were slivers or tiny deposits of coal dust that only burrowed deeper when they were poked and pried at with needles and tweezers. Anybody could see that. Not many asked him anything beyond how he was or what was he up to these days.

With his shrug and a leisurely sip from whatever he was drinking he erased any number of unsettling questions from his mind. Mornings he drank coffee flavoured with a drowned gingersnap and a splash of rye. After noon he switched to beer, a finger of this, a finger of that. 'This' was usually scotch and 'that' was usually rye. The beer, he said, was good for his stomach.

Helps the digestive system like a week of rhubarb.

But that light beer, he said, was just plain tap-water that he could get for free out of his own kitchen sink. I don't have to pay a lousy two eighty-five for a bottle of water, you know.

So the beer he drank was dark and bitter, brewed faster with all the damned chemicals these days, but what can you do: it's all piss water anyway.

He said those things: strong men were built like brick shit-houses. If something was true he said it was sure as shit. Bad coal-miners—work mates named Sleepy or Fats or Candles (if his nose ran)—were men who couldn't dig their way out of an outhouse. A gentleman was a man who wouldn't say shit if his mouth was full of it. And his own wife, the woman who disappeared from his sight like one of his hidden bottles—a little too hidden, but around here some place, goddamn it—Sera, the woman who left only him to remember her by, Sera, he said, was a woman full of piss and vinegar.

If she'd had any schooling she'd have been a holy terror. More guts than a slaughter-house.

Pep had the gift for reducing everything he knew and everything he was to its most simple, ungarnished truth: shit. All things, he said, even himself, especially himself, become fertilizer in the end. Remember that, boy. Food for daisies; food for thought.

He liked that idea. You could see that. Once you die, you die: end of story. He wasn't sure if he felt more or less responsibility by not believing in the human spirit, being entirely on his own and wanting it that way. In fact, the only souls he claimed to see came from cracking open a bottle of beer.

Here I am, waiting to die at the goddamn end of the world. Bring on the worms.

In the main, he kept to himself all those years, minding his own business, or minding his own bloody business, as he liked to say, and the only time he was seen was when he stepped carefully into the day from a tavern's darkness.

Nobody ever saw him going in.

*

Darkness. Celi feels darkness with every sense but sight. He is inside a mountain, propped against a wall of coal and the floor, hard and littered with debris. His hands are cool. His mouth is dry, dusty, but he is sweating; his whole body is soaked. His clothes would cling to his skin if they were not wool. And there is silence, a calm, misleading silence that muffles his breath pushing through the air and his heart pumping blood to his head. The darkness muffles the sweat dribbling white worms down his face. It smothers the sound of water that scribbles down the tunnel's ribs. The darkness dissolves all other sounds like the inside of a sea shell, or an ear. Celi reaches out, extending an arm he isn't sure is there— the air feels too warm against his skin, too similar to the temperature of his own blood. But he pushes his hand through the darkness, sweeps large arcs away from his face, touching and grasping nothing. When he brings back the arm, he feels in the palm of his hand to find, with his other hand, that it is numb. His skin is both gritty and smooth, the same sort of way his hands became changing a truck's oil. But more than that, the hand feels black, as if he has touched the darkness and sunk his hand into its colour. Bleeding, he thinks, as he clasps the hand under his other armpit. His head-lamp died quickly, he remembers. The pinprick of light was snuffed by two great, dark fingers. He made for the tunnel, and fell. Now, there seems little point in moving. As if his numb hand had grasped sleep itself and pulled him toward it, Celi's mind slips into the darkness, sinking without a sound. His eyes close—there is no difference from when they are open—and he sleeps.

*

A younger Celi was once walking by himself through an orchard of bergamot trees. It was late in the day. The sun, pointing elsewhere, had long left southern Italy—known by most Italians as the land of midday. The day was past, but there was still enough light to see where he was going. The trees in front of him looked hard and black, with few shoots. Each branch curved toward its fruit, as if searching for the green bergamots instead of bearing them.

Suddenly, he heard the sound of birds, what seemed like hundreds of birds, chirping all at the same time. Celi squinted into the nearby trees but saw nothing. The sound had stopped and the branches were empty, twisted. They cast still more twisted shadows onto the ground in front of him.

In one of those shadows Celi saw a round shape, about the size of a hat. He looked up for a nest that he knew must be above him, but he couldn't place where the shadow fell from. The branches were too dark. The leaves were too dull a green. And looking down at the ground, he saw that it was just as difficult to follow the lines of light and shadow that curled away from the shadow-nest.

Still, he didn't give up. Celi knew that a couple of birds could be sold in town, no matter what they were: nightingales, sparrows, owls, blackbirds, even crows. He usually went night-fowling with a lantern, catching robins, serins, finches and wrens on moonless, windy nights. The birds were especially easy to grab because they took refuge on low branches and tucked their heads under a wing to avoid the wind. They never heard or saw his approach. An open sack in one hand, he simply knocked the birds over with the other and they were his.

But you take them whenever you find them, thought Celi. Night or day. The birds would bring him a new sickle or maybe a pig that he could raise and sell for even more money.

He looked at the shadow-nest once again. Then he went

to each tree to see which one pointed its shadow toward the spot. But not even the trees betrayed the birds. They held the shadow-nest together, confusing him so entirely that even their trunks seemed to send away different-angled shadows. Some of the shadows shot directly at the nest, others arched away, but all of them returned with several branches to guard the shadow-birds. Each branch twisted into another, overlapping both its arms and his uncertainty. Within half an hour the sun too abandoned him and he was forced to walk the rest of the way home in darkness.

That night Celi had a dream that turned into the most beautiful nightmare he'd ever seen. Again, he was walking home through the bergamot trees. He heard the same cry of birds and stopped in the same place only to listen to the same silence when he looked for the birds.

He was surprised, in his dream, to find a lone fig tree not far from where he'd stood that afternoon. Apparently, he'd been so busy following shadows and bergamot branches that he hadn't noticed the figs. How strange, he thought, because the two types of trees were completely different from one another. Fig branches didn't twist; they arched upward like an open palm, fingers spread wide. He couldn't tell what kind of figs they were: *bianchi, melanzani, catalani* or *inverniticbi.* Once again, the sun was going down and the light was scarce.

But when he looked between the branches of the tree, he thought he saw a dark shape forming in the sky. The shape flew toward the tree, growing larger as it approached. Floating or gliding, it looked like the biggest bird he'd ever seen, as big as the tree itself. In fact, it flapped its wings so slowly that Celi was amazed such a large bird could stay in the sky at all.

He soon saw that the shape was not one bird but many. There were hundreds of birds—a huge flock that flew in the formation of a single bird. He watched them with wide, unblinking eyes and an open mouth as they navigated the up-

and-down motion of one bird flapping two incredibly large wings.

The large bird drew closer to the fig tree, hanging above it for a moment, then gracefully touched down on the tree's highest branch. Some of the small birds in the formation actually sat on the fig tree, but the rest of the birds hovered above and maintained the image of a single bird. It was brown and grey, with darker hues along the creases of its wings. A few white breast-feathers on each small bird gave the larger one a speckled appearance.

Celi didn't breathe. He thought the least noise would break the birds apart and scare them from the tree. Still, he was curious. The huge bird was so lifelike. It loomed over him, scanning the nearby treetops and the ground below as if searching for worms the size of dogs. He wondered which would notice him first: the large bird or the small birds that made up its image. Quietly, with the utmost care, he took a step toward them. He looked down—quickly—to avoid a twig, a rock or something that might snap, but he was too late. He stepped on something dark and round that made a crunching noise under his foot.

When he jerked his leg up, he saw there was nothing on the ground but a shadow: the shadow of a nest. Celi swung his head up to look at the fig tree and saw that the huge bird was now studying him. Its feathers were darker, rougher than before, because even the smaller birds were pointing their dark beaks at Celi. And all at once the image disappeared.

The birds scattered into a thousand different directions, escaping through the fig tree's wide, open fingers. A second later the birds were back. They flocked above him in a stormy mass, chirping so wildly that he had to cover his ears with both hands. He could do nothing but crouch under their seeming weight. When the birds rose above him in the shape of a white, speckled fist, he woke from his dream with a shout.

Celi believed in dreams, just enough to be wary of them.

So the next day, he went to see a Bagnarota. She was older than most—a good sign, he thought. The woman lived in a small house next to the rocks that cut the town in half. She wasn't pleased to see him, but then most women who had the gift of sight put on a suspicious face for strangers. He'd brought her a chicken to bridge their meeting, but she tossed it in her kitchen and let the bird walk free.

Mi faciti nu favuri? he asked politely.

But she brushed him off with a wave, as if to say: What do you want from me?

With her right hand the Bagnarota pulled at her eyelid and stretched it away from her eye. When she let go, the skin stayed bunched up like a broken basket. He was tempted to leave, but she'd begun examining him with the eye.

He told her about the bergamot trees, about the sound of birds and about the shadow he'd seen. He didn't tell her why he'd wanted to find the birds, or anything about his night-fowling. But the dream seemed the most interesting to her ears. She straightened up and her eyelid smoothed over again, so that it was simply lined with wrinkles.

You will find what you are looking for at night, said the woman. In your dream or awake, it makes no difference. Now get out of my house before I piss on you and tell you your future.

Celi might have run from the house except for one thing: he was young. The Bagnarota didn't frighten him as much as she might have frightened a boy who was afraid of town witches, or an older man who knew better than to stay. Youth gave him confidence. He was strong, a good worker. There were few who could keep up with that kind of youth. Even when Celi herded sheep he would push his body to its limits. Given a field to plough or harvest, he covered every handkerchief of land with the same measured strength from beginning to end. While other men brought homemade pagnotta loaves stuffed with fried peppers and crushed olives, Celi took no lunch, except for a giant lemon that he ate with salt, washed down with yellow bluebell stalks for water.

As for the Bagnarota, he decided, she could give him a moment more for so plump a chicken.

Perhaps I would like to hear my future, he said.

She snapped at him: Every death of the Pope I hear those words. The last time was fifteen years ago, and yet they never surprise me. Like all the others, you don't know what you want: perhaps yes, perhaps no, but always perhaps. Perhaps you can come back when you find out, or perhaps not.

Celi's only reaction was to smile.

Goodbye perhaps, she said, turning away from him.

He wasn't sure if she'd turned her back to challenge his conviction or forget about him, but he didn't care for her riddle. Celi left the house without giving her another word.

He decided to return to the bergamot orchard, of course. Waiting for a dream about birds seemed more difficult than finding an actual nest in a real orchard. But this time he went at night, on a windy night when he could find the birds sitting low on the branches. On this particular night, the moon was his lantern. Strangely, the wind hadn't spoiled the sky. He brought only a cotton sack and a walnut stick with him so that he could either grab the birds or knock them down into the bag.

As he walked he thought back to the Bagnarota. He'd heard how fearless they were, so the old woman he'd met hadn't really shocked him. Some people said that even their tongues bit a man. But then most of those rumours were only gossip: *voce* or *maldicenza*. In fact, he knew many men who were more bitter than she. It wasn't uncommon to see an unlucky man—whose mule was dying, or whose wagon was broken—cursing the heavens. However, the Bagnarota hadn't been half as coarse as that. *Lassamu perdiri*, thought Celi: Leave it to be lost. He would find out for himself what the birds and his dream meant.

The bergamot trees were easy to find. He'd walked past them a hundred times on fifty given days. Often, he'd gone night-fowling in the same area, so he knew the land well. A sharp, solitary cry of birds announced his presence in the orchard, but the wind turned the noise into more of a wail.

The last thing he expected to see was a woman. She sat in the very spot where he'd found the shadow-nest, not far from a number of bergamot trees and a fig tree that held the moon in its hand. She wore a white dress with a dark cape and she sat with her arms wrapped around her knees. Celi couldn't see her face because it was resting in her arms and turned in the other direction.

His first thought was that she was lost. She was crying. It was her shriek that the wind had hurled through the forest. To save time, she'd cut through the orchard, and become confused when darkness fell. The wind wouldn't have helped her either. Celi could hear it whistling as it spiraled along the bergamot branches.

Salute, Celi said, from a distance.

Despite his effort not to startle her, she flinched from his voice.

But her beauty surprised him more than he had surprised her. She was uncommonly beautiful, with large eyes and a generous, full mouth. Her hair was brown, he thought. Even with the moon's help, he couldn't quite tell.

Don't worry, he said quickly, it's only me—I mean, I didn't want to frighten you.

Her eyes were wide; they were staring at him. He dropped his sack and stick to the ground. Then he walked toward her. When he was close enough touch her shoulder, he bent down beside the girl. But it was she who reached for him. Her cape spread wide as her arms left her knees and reached out.

Celi automatically opened his arms to comfort her. In the

flash of a second he was ready to feel her warmth, or—more likely—warm her with his. But he wasn't prepared for her weight, pushing him down. And his eyes were closed when he felt the first brush of feathers across his cheek.

*

Celi's own gasp jars him from the dream. He is breathing hard, the memory of suffocation still fresh in his thoughts. There are other things to think about, he tells himself, besides air. Pep is coming. There are other things to think about.

*

Pep was always the first to go in. Pep was first to enter a mine before every morning shift began. Every day but Sunday he left his house, near the end of a tired, defeated street, paved now, without gutters. The street was wide enough to make a U-turn with a mule cart. Pep said the town measured and planned all the streets in Frank by a mule's capacity to change directions. And somehow that fit—even if he was lying.

This was the Italian district. Dagotown. A group of houses built tight, squeezed into twenty-five-foot lots, all of them one to four feet apart and slightly angled, spilling foundation corners and room splinters into their neighbours' properties like frustrated elbows fighting for an armrest. Rainwater fell on one house, slid down the walls of another and was bailed into a third. Coal dust from each stove chimney mushroomed and joined the collective black billows hovering over the street and the nearby mine tipple. And a sneeze from one home brought a muttered *salute*, or more often an unconscious wipe of the nose, from its neighbour, the *casa del vicino*.

Today, one flush rang through the whole wayward line of houses like a voice—a curse, some *maladittu*—in a string tied between two tin cans. The voice ended at Pep's house, where Pep, bucking the trend of indoor plumbing, used an outhouse right into the eighties. Sera might not have wanted a 'shit-house' inside her house and Pep—one got the feeling—would never have pressed her to change, even after she left, or went missing.

All this was guesswork, hearsay and the stuff of jigsaws. Sera was a proud old lady, said the few remaining neighbours who knew her. They didn't need reminding that she was barely thirty when she disappeared, before the whole town started disappearing. They had little to say to Pep over the years and even less to remember. Why should they know how old she was?

Those peasant women from the old country, toughened by rolling the earth and bread and babies, milking sheep and goats and themselves, could look ancient at fifteen. They seemed to live past two hundred by holding onto their wiry grey hair, their wrinkled foreheads, their widow's peaks and their crow's-foot eyes for an entire eighty years. This was *their* secret, the thing they held onto with both wrinkled hands. It gave them dignity.

But Sera wasn't like that. If it wasn't money, then something else kept her youth intact. Pride perhaps. She wasn't old, she didn't look old, and she couldn't have seemed old, except in mind. Stubborn maybe, but she was smart enough to want to leave this God-forsaken place for something better, somewhere where you could breathe your own dust-free air next to your own noiseless house.

They lived in this house, a cottage really, at the far corner of the street, in practically the furthest corner of the town (at the bottom of a bluff), backed up against an alley and a grassy hill, in what has always been called Dagotown, but before that—before anything, before even 'always'—it was called the swamp. The first surveyors of the area slept in tents, clearing flies from their dinner plates and living more than two winters only if they cooked their own food. Later, Dagotown became the swamp's nickname (the *soprannome*, in Italian), a name that covered the real one so completely nobody remembered what they first called the community.

The hill gave a natural incline to the back yard, a gentle slope that brushed up against the house and veered off to the sides. There was an obvious pattern in the earth, a set of swirls that were now grass-covered and weed-ridden like bald-headed prairie. Sera must have tilled the ground into a labyrinth of water canals, with vegetables planted along the crests. Meandering like liquid scribbles across a dirt page, a bucket of water poured at the far end could make its journey through the entire garden, watering everything just enough to keep it alive for another week.

Pep couldn't have thought of that. Either he didn't know how to garden or he gave up on it after Sera left. The only thing still alive was the rhubarb, perennial and immortal, close to the house at the end, or the beginning, of the garden's maze.

There wasn't much else to see. The street was the same, maybe a little modernized by the façade of pavement but still waiting for some wayward mules. The houses were the same, minus most of their inhabitants but still crooked and ready to echo a ghost's sneeze to the end of the street.

Pep's house stood brown and peeling in a weak September sun barely warm enough to feel with an open palm. The house looked soft and blurred, worn around the edges by ancient gritty winds that blew coal dust from the mine. The curtains were grey and sagged from hooks inside three narrow front windows. There was a miniature veranda, too small for more than a chair, that cut a wobbly line from the house to the street. No sidewalk. No people.

The front lawn was small, practically an afterthought to the builder, who didn't want to drag the lumber into the middle of the lot. Maybe the mules couldn't turn that sharply.

Or perhaps Pep built it and forgot to plan for more space.

The only remarkable thing about the house was the strange patch of brilliant green grass that sat like a stool in the middle of the lawn, three feet from the veranda. Even though there were thick strands of grass bending over in huge arcs to touch the surrounding area, the patch remained perfectly round, a tall emerald circle that broke to sunburnt brown and met the pavement.

Pep walked from his door toward the green patch. He was bent over like the grass; if straightened by force his back would surely break. He said he was sixty-eight, but he was probably much older, perhaps by ten years or more. He wore the same hat as usual: black, with a black band. He carried a brown leather grip. The bag could open like a wheezing accordion, but in Pep's hand it looked solid, bobbing gently, like a birdhouse. Fifty years ago the bag might well have contained birds, canaries used to check the levels of gas in the mine, but today there was only a ham-on-rye sandwich, a thermos of coffee and some gingersnaps.

Despite the morning sun and the clear sky, Pep wore a thick, dark jacket, once blue. He didn't bother to zip it up. His black trousers hung low on his hips and whispered—as he walked—against the green grass.

*

From what Pep remembered after roughly thirty-five years, the first thing that Sera did in Canada was put the house together. Though he had survived with his own practical method of living alone, with only his mother's ghost to help him, Sera decided to create some life in the house so that its vitality could be seen even from the outside, like the seeds on a strawberry.

She started by taking all of his tools that he always left on the counter, and dumped them in the nearest kitchen drawer. She thought that he wouldn't be completely disoriented by the new change. But as she moved she gathered both momentum and courage. She got rid of the tin pie-plates that he used for dishes and bought real plates and saucers, filling up Pep's bare kitchen cabinets. Serviettes and place-mats replaced recycled newspapers and, getting bolder as she progressed, she threw out his seventeen-year-old mug, his *only* mug-glass-shaving-cup in the whole house, without a moment's thought. She sprinkled crushed eggshells on the wooden rails of every stubborn drawer. She repaired the fridge handle and removed the screwdriver that was wedged in the door to open it; once inside, she garbaged jar after jar of pickled relics no longer fit for goats. Dish soap replaced Pep's practical bar of hand soap by the faucet and shocking-white curtains now hung above the sink in place of a sunbeam. Almost every change was completely new to him: doilies on the table between meals; chopped-up flowers and dried leaves in garlic jars; shades for every bare-assed lightbulb; homespun linen that was never used, yet filled every other drawer in the house; olive oil on every hinge, squeaky or not; the basement stairs page-white.

And through all of the changes Pep left her completely alone, shaking his head in amazement and quietly laughing at each new discovery his eyes and nostrils found.

Really, it was Sera who discovered *him* during the organizing. Every scratch and stain, every brush of his body against the house taught her about his quiet bachelorhood, his energy-efficient life, aesthetically bare yet as personal as a signature on a blank, tan canvas. He hid his extra liquor below the sink beside a pail of potatoes and a bottle of vinegar (his only household cleaner). He ironed his shirts with the bottom of his coffee pot, leaving brown rings on most of them. When he ironed too aggressively he left coffee stains; when he ironed too slowly he left burn marks; the rest of the time he left coal-dust smudges and ash marks from the soot that flew up around the burner and settled all over the kitchen. But with the other appliances he was strangely careful: he kept every lamp and appliance safely unplugged. Every day he sat in the same wooden chair that faced the door and the coal stove so that he could guard both. His other chairs may have been towel rests, but by the looks of them he'd had few guests. The seats were dusty and lacked the polish of human use. The rifle butt of a well-oiled over-and-under left the only shine mark on the floor, by a corner door that led to the bedroom.

Sera saw that he had owned a dog with long brown fur; she found traces of fur near his bed and deep scratches on both sides of the back door. She examined everything, every detail, and learned about her husband just as if she had been there all those years, in that tiny kitchen, watching him open the screen door for the dog with his left hand and remain sitting only by stretching his arm across the room and flicking the catch with a single finger. Again, it was the house that told her that story: over the course of a dog's life he had scratched corresponding grooves into the door's metal frame with his watch. His well-worn tracks over the same linoleum path, from one side of the bed to the kitchen to the other side of the bed beside the dresser to the kitchen door and back again in reverse order, completely re-created his past for her eyes, showing her his frugal life before she existed.

Her last discovery was the most telling. She found a flock of her own letters stored in a box with a perfumed rabble of others. They were hidden deep at the back of a basement shelf with, predictably, some old rifle bolts. Both the letters and the bolts were safely out of sight. Above all, she resented the letters she had written him being clustered together with those from other women. She didn't like them lying in the same horizontal pile, like bread slices or conquests, ordered by time instead of importance.

So she waited for Pep to get home from the mine and sit

himself carefully on the edge of his chair before she came up from the basement and walked into the front room with the box high on her hand, like a waiter delivering the bill.

But there was more to it than that: when Sera was a child her father would give her a large glass of water just to watch her walk with it to the table. She'd carry the glass high in one hand above her head, as if the further away from the ground, the less likely it was to spill. Of course, she carried Pep's letters the same unblinking way. Except she walked past him.

Dressed in a plain beige housedress (that she normally would never leave the house in), Pep's plaid-red hunting jacket and a pair of practical green slippers, Sera opened the winter door and then the screen door and walked out into the snow.

There was something strangely ceremonial about the whole thing, and Pep thought at first that she was kidding him, walking prouder than the widows from Bagnara, Calabria, who float through the markets with huge bowls of fruit and bundles of fish on their heads, towing still prouder children with bundles of their own. Her distant gaze and fixed mouth made him question his own eyes as soon as she disappeared from his sight. She hadn't even looked at him. When he made it to the door she was already kneeling in the snow, her back to him, jacket open and winged by hidden elbows. She looked huge and powerful, hunched in the snow with the box of letters beside her.

But he knew better than to follow her outside, able to forecast her quiet hurricane without walking right into it. Seeing her there, hunched over, spread wide and threatening to fly away, may have felt like the first drop of rain on the tip of his nose.

With bare hands Sera dug at the snow in front of her. Then she brushed away the ice crystals that clung to the brown, frozen grass. When she straightened up and took a box of matches from her pocket Pep went around the corner and watched from the window, leaving a series of nose prints that Sera would later clean.

She would clean them with a smile.

She didn't crumple the first letters that she put into the pit. She simply stacked them on one another, each letter's folds accepting the other's in silent congruence. Some of the matches were burnt already, used months before when Pep darkened his new moustache with the blackened tips. He'd wanted to avoid hearing 'hey bumfuzz' from the other miners.

Sera threw the used matches onto the letters for kindling and began lighting corners. There were few flames, but she could tell the fire was sufficiently ignited by the brown tide that curled each page, ebbed for a moment and curled again. When the flames finally took, Sera locked her fingers together and watched the first wisps of white smoke slither up into the cold air like a rope. She sat down in the snow, crossed her legs and felt herself sinking, the heat of her bottom melting another hole in the snow.

She fed the fire one letter at a time. With her left hand she reached inside the box and, keeping her eyes on the fire, passed each letter to her right hand. The letters then floated down into the flames, each sheet of paper burning in the middle before landing on the writhing stack, red as the skirts that only married women wore in Castrovilla, paler than the bloody veins in a Sicilian orange.

Sera breathed in the smoke, coughing at first, but enjoying the heat in her lungs mixing with the February air, breathing the letters themselves, reading them all with her lungs and coughing up the odd one that wasn't from her. With blackened shreds of words swarming around her, she tasted the letters on her lips and imagined them swirling in her chest, reforming to make symbols that a doctor would X-ray and look up from his projector, baffled. Exhaling bubbles of burnt words, she could push whole black sentences out of her mouth, silent yet understood.

Even the pain of breathing the letters felt good to her. The curls of smoke brought a sharpness that she wanted to remember, always. When she sucked the letters in quickly, her throat felt raw, stripped clean by the word-smoke. She coughed occasionally because the cold air mixed with the words and broke them into thorny paragraphs. It was that mixture of cold air and smouldering words that cracked her teeth, she decided, or made her mouth too numb to feel teeth or spoken words. Both thoughts sent a smile to her face; she would be smiling for weeks, grinning like a jagged-toothed pumpkin, or have candle wax for a tongue. It didn't really matter which happened.

She felt tears on her face and shifted backward to relieve her eyes from the smoke. But when she closed her eyes and turned her head from side to side she saw the flame centred in her vision. Wherever she looked, with open or clenched eyelids, the red flame remained.

*

In his first letters to Sera, Pep described two things: flowers and money. The talk about the money he earned was to pacify Sera's father, Massimo, who he knew was reading the letters aloud to his whole family. The old man naturally assumed the letters were for everybody, as much for his friends in the cheese factory as for Sera, since he was the head of the family in the town to which this young Italian from America was addressing so much news. The flower descriptions were for Sera, some petals even included, flattened and mummified, in the folds of his letters. Pep thought that a woman would like to know about flowers, or could appreciate their beauty more than he could, so he simply told her their colours and their Canadian names, hoping that Sera would fall in love with the sound of the words in her father's mouth. He didn't learn until much later that Massimo passed the letters to Sera as soon as his tongue struggled over the first hint of English, refusing to drag himself any further across a word with so many vowels and no one consistent way of pronouncing them all.

He knew only one English phrase, and practised it every time he heard an English word, just before he gravely left the room, his fingers of his right hand curled and touching each other, holding an imaginary thought in the air: *Eye musta to piss.*

Despite her father, Sera fell in love, reading the English words and then passing Pep's letters back to Massimo. The whole family—aunts, uncles, cousins, nieces and nephews— listened to stories about Canadian snapdragons, shooting stars, buttercups, tiger lilies and roosterheads. *This one is called the head of a rooster because it is floppy and red and crows when plucked from the ground.* Even daisies excited her because Pep told her that they were named after the sun— the day's eye—and the English language became something magical that made her father leave the room after the first vowel.

Pep may have researched the names or made them up; Sera didn't know where he learned the words. His letters told her that sunflowers weren't 'turn to the sun' or *girasole*, as they were in Italian. In English, *girasole* became Jerusalem, a name that other travellers had carried with them to pollinate even the cities between Italy and Canada—between her and him. Carnations, he said, were made from the ragged edges of raw meat: *carne.*

Other times Pep sent bubble gum instead of flowers with his letters and Sera's family chewed to the sound of Canadian stories, Massimo imagining the fortune a coal-miner could find in America, Sera imagining the fortune of marrying a coal-miner in America, and all of the nieces and nephews imagining the bubble gum found in the coal-mines of America. Everyone knew that America was a place for the *fortunati. Trovare America*, they said, find America. The words were the same as saying, find your fortune. And for Sera the meaning was no different.

She had never considered leaving Italy but it took less than twelve letters for her to begin sniffing the envelopes to smell America. In the letters without bubble gum she breathed in a grainy dryness, the smell of an old chestnut pan, but she had no way of knowing that it was coal dust. The particles were so small they never showed up against the paper's whiteness. Unknowingly, Pep rubbed the dust into the fibres as his hand moved across the paper. He wrote with his right hand, the page turned almost sideways so that he filled each line by piling the words on one another, as if he were stacking boxes to see over a very high ledge into Sera's heart.

Because of her father's example, Sera could only imagine Pep's tongue twisting, straining across his teeth, as if he were unable to write a word without tasting it first, mashing each word against the roof of his mouth before he let it escape his clenched fingers.

Sera's letters were demurely shorter than Pep's, with the daily news of city officials imprisoned for stealing garbage to feed their pigs, a Calabrese hilltop town of Greek ancestry that refused to speak Italian or a soccer match against the rival Messina *circolo* that ended, surprisingly, without a fight among the spectators. Her longest letter was barely two pages, describing Bagnara's patron saint, recently dunked into the Mediterranean. Hopefully, she'd written, he will come to his senses and improve the town's luck. But mixed into her news, there was always a word or two that made Pep jump up and mash Canadian flowers and leaves and ants and clumps of dirt and bubble gum into his nearest envelopes—things she imagined he would like to see or taste, or a friend she knew he would like to meet, just the smallest hint that told him she thought about him during her day. And that was enough.

Her tiny letters to him could have been typed, had typewriters existed. Each word was carefully crafted. She wrote in Italian, of course, feeling too self-conscious to write in English—and though the pages were few, they lasted him hours as he imagined her hand—he could see it—moving slowly across the page. He watched her thumb as it gripped the belly of a feather, probably. He watched her waiting for an idea to swim its way from her heart to her fingertips without a breath and burst with relief over two or three words at once. Her fingers shifted up and slightly left, then right to stretch for the first letter in his full name at the top of the page, *Caro Giuseppe.* Then he saw those fingers relax into a careful calligraphy until she came to her name at the end, swinging the 'S' just as wildly as his 'G.' Most times, her thoughts seemed so careful that he could only imagine Sera picking lint from her sweater. Her words were distant and chosen.

And Pep worried about them all, all the words she deliberately avoided and all the meaning he extracted, with the puzzled look of a beginning pianist, unsure of the sounds he was discovering, or perhaps inventing. But at the end of each letter she wished him well, hoped to hear from him soon and penned her full name, *Serafina,* in that scrawled flurry of movement which left Pep dizzy and euphoric for the next month between letters. He came to know that she was just as anxious as he was.

*

With her back still to Pep, Sera faced the street, and curtained neighbours watched her preparing some kind of campfire. Mrs. Arabiato washed the inside of her windows four times that day, even though the scene wasn't so strange to her eyes. With natural gas heaters newly installed in many Crowsnest houses, some people were driven from their reeking homes when basement-hung deer and moose began to rot and fester. Tents and small shacks appeared in their front and back yards, and the only ones who seemed not to suffer were the men who spent their days in the mine, their money in the bars and only their sleeping hours under their own stinking roofs. The women, however, were less sympathetic to the smell, and Sera (cooking something in the snow) was seen as just another wife chased out of her house by her husband's winter kill.

So began their happy union, with a veritable bonfire in front of the house and the Crowsnest wind rapidly blowing all of the ashes away, back to the probable owners of the letters. Sera recovered her own letters, for the ones she didn't inhale the mountain winds brought back, along with a steady layering of ash and coal dust that coated every dish and table, framing even the frames of pictures so that they could never be taken from the white rectangles they began to hide, and covering even the house's inhabitants so they looked far more Moorish than Italian.

Sera almost never minded the dust. Only when she forgot about the letters that she had burnt and the ashes flying into the air did she curse the wind, curses in every colour muttered in dialect to some ever-present listener to her thoughts. Her typical monologue was short and answered a question Pep never asked, yet was somehow made to regret. She might enter the kitchen with a broom in her hand, find him prodding some boiled potatoes and respond:

No, no, no, no, she said, I will never be so comfortable with that prick of a wind I will want to shake hands with it, I don't care what you say.

A healthy nod of agreement was his best and only real defence. Other times Pep would be the one who walked into the room where she was working, covered in a grey fog of dust, beating the couch with a flyswatter, scrubbing the tiles or examining a picture against the window's light.

What do I say to the wind and his dust, Sera answered his silent question, I say here, here's my message, and she opened the door, hiked up her skirt with one hand and pulled it around so that the day's eye could witness the full potency of her hate.

She was a remarkable woman by any standards, Pep decided in those beginning weeks, though he quickly learned to close the door and the drapes in the front of the house before he left for the mine. Whatever Sera believed about the dust and the ghosts of cremated letters, the sun was not as all-seeing as their neighbours.

Pep knew about superstitions, and the brown patch of dirt in the front yard where Sera burned the letters changed to grass by midsummer, an ominously brighter green than the rest of the lawn.

TWO

Something brushes against his face, scraping him awake.
Celi's eyes are suddenly open but the room is still dark. His
mouth is dry, so when he tries to speak, all that comes out is
a hoarse groan. But the groan is enough to startle the
someone else right beside him into screeching back. (Then
there is silence.) It is so incredibly quiet, the silence, like
swimming under water. And just as incredible: even the
timbers have stopped creaking. The mixture of rocking-chair
wails from the tunnel's thousands of stilts has ceased.
Whatever coal dust was in the air from the last shift has now
settled to the ground. Besides a dull and distant hum of fresh
air being pumped into the mine, the only other ripple of
movement comes from the push of Celi's breath. *Who's that?*
Echoing through the tunnel, Celi's voice, and others, break
the calm like a smooth stone. For a moment he thinks all he's
heard is the echo from his first waking groan, but the feeling
that someone has passed by him is too strong. Hopeful
somehow, he casts still more words into the darkness: Jesus
Christ you scared the shit outta me. Who's there? *Who's there?*
shimmers through the tunnel. And then another voice, ten
feet away, does come from the dark: *My name's Fina, it's
Fina. Who's that?* The voice is young, a boy's voice,
unbroken and almost girlish. Christ, what are you, a bucker,
what the hell are you doing here? *I just came in. The light
went.* What tunnel are you supposed to be in? *I don't know.
I can't remember.* Shit. That's great. Just great. (There is a

long pause, the sound of methane threading through darkness, before either says anything more.) I'm Celi. I was
checking some of the gas levels before closing up. I thought
I had at least four more tunnel's worth in my lamp, until I hit
a pocket. Big surprise. Then I get found by you. (Another
pause.) You best sit yourself down, kid. It's gonna be a long
wait. I don't reckon anybody to come for us till the morning
shift comes in. That's when the levels get checked again,
before the first shift. Then they'll see our tags are missing and
start the search. Until then, here we are. *Can't you find your
way out?* No sense in it. I'm telling you: the only way out is
to wait for someone with a light. You're damned lucky you
didn't fall down a chute and break your pecker or maybe
something important. Christ, if I hadn't got stuck in this
damned place you surely would have. Tonight I was finishing
up, putting in some extra time that isn't on the regular board,
but they'll see your tag's missing right away. Don't worry
about that none. Between the end of this shift and the start
of the next one they'll figure it out all right. It won't be long
after that. I thought I might be stuck here a little longer, seeing
as my tag's not with the usual ones, but with you here we're
sittin' pretty. Just relax. (They are silent for a moment, Celi
shaking his head in the dark at his dumb luck.) *Who'll come
for us then?* Fire boss at first, or maybe one of the pit bosses,
getting ready to sort out their tunnel plans. The straw bosses
don't get here until they've got their fresh horses teamed up,
figured out which ones are going where . . . but the first guy
to open up, count off the tags as the men come out would be
Pep, Pep Rogolino. Mornings he comes in, farts around.
That's all they got him doing these days. If he doesn't notice
the missing tags right off then one of the others will, sometime
later. Nothing to worry about, though. We'll hear them
bumping into things before too long, on their way up the
slope to their rooms. Hell, once a year this happens to some
bozo asleep at the switch. Tonight we bust your cherry.

Happened to me once before so leastways you're lucky. You got yourself a tour guide. Celi hopes his voice is calming the bucker. The last thing he needs is for the kid to start running for the entrance: nobody will find him then. He sounds all right though, maybe a little quiet. Celi doesn't want to ask him how he is. That would only start him thinking about it, and get him wondering, if he isn't wondering already. As for Celi's hand, it's starting to feel normal again. The numbing's gone. He tried not to make much of scratches or minor injuries, ever since he heard a miner shrug off a severed finger with the words: Well, that's one less to stick up my ass at the end of the day. Celi knew the man didn't believe what he'd said about the missing finger, but he said it to help the rest of the men somehow. Everybody loses something, thinks Celi. It only gets worse when you lose it alone.

*

Pep was eleven.

His first job in the mine was bucking coal down the chutes toward rail cars that ran through the tunnels. Miners, black as a murder of crows, shovelled the rocks away from the gassy face toward the chute. Their shovels and picks scraped the walls and the floor as they burrowed deeper into the seam, stopping only to wait for dripping water to settle the dust. From where Pep stood, inside a carved closet next to a timber, he could twist his head around the corner and watch a soft black cloud tumbling continuously. The men were invisible, shadows at most, behind rolling fog. Chunks of coal bubbled out and rolled toward him. Then the coal fell down a hole the size of a kitchen table. More of a funnel than anything else, the chute clogged six times an hour and the buckers kicked, prodded and jumped on the heaps, forcing them back open, for a dollar a day.

Behind him the bratticemen erected partitions and

controlled the air into Pep's passage, into his tunnel. They sent a cool breeze up past him, but he stood out of its way, sucking in deeply only when he felt light-headed, the methane swirling too near his nostrils.

Sometimes using a lever or a pitchfork, Pep stabbed the mounds of coal, twisting the pole until the chute wedged open and the coal dropped into the cars thirty to forty feet below him. He tested the piles with the same hesitancy that he used on his mother's spaghetti Bolognese, prying his fork from side to side, moving his head with the motion of the fork to keep his head-lamp focused on his work.

A pinprick of light was all he needed to see. After the first two weeks he was so comfortable with a reflector dish on his head that he seemed unable to move his eyeballs, even in daylight, without swivelling his neck and the imaginary head-lamp. Only when the chute was too blocked to use his fork did he jump on the chunks of coal, like the rest of the buckers, leaping for the edge as soon as the chute threatened to swallow him.

*

But his mining started even earlier. When he was five, a neighbour caught Pep eating pieces of dirt in the yard on a bet—kiss Rhonda Carpi or lick the ground—but his mother, Teresa, simply sent the woman outside carrying a fork.

If he is going to eat dirt, he may as well do it properly.

Seven years later Pep started smoking cigarettes with a fork, so that Teresa would never see or smell the nicotine stains on his fingers. He had used forks all his life, he thought, prying at the coal with a much larger fork; no reason to get her knickers in a knot.

A year after that he gave up the smoking altogether. Lung-tired at thirteen, he switched to chewing Macdonald tobacco in the mine to make himself spit the dust from his mouth. Most of the miners did that.

The coal that Pep wedged free bashed its way down the coal chutes into mine cars that were railed, tagged and dumped again, moved past tippers, timbermen, tunnellers, fire bosses, pit bosses, haulers, dinky-drivers, gandy-dancers, picking tables and gravity screens, the coal sorted then by size and grade and finally loaded into railway cars to God-knows-where; Pep didn't know. He skirted all of the movement, trying to just stay out of the way, yet not completely sure of what way that was.

*

Their first night together was more of a relief for Sera than anything else. Pep was feeling the combined aftermath of a chaotic day, the late hour, too many *aperitivi*, too much homemade wine, champagne, Sardinian grappa and *digestivi* to be much good to her. Shame made her leave on a white camisole, slip and stockings, yet Pep barely found his way out of the bathroom to see her.

His mother, however, had done the pre-checking. As soon as Sera was settled in her room, changing after the long trip, Teresa made the pretence of bringing in one more towel for her. The old bitch got an eyeful, a protective nosiness that Sera would remember the rest of her life: the time her mother-in-law came to find out just what her son was getting.

It was hard to tell if she was disappointed or just acting busy. She bustled into the room with a question on her lips—immediately forgotten—the very moment Sera was in her underclothes.

Scusa, Teresa seemed to say, so casually. Then she folded the towel—far too carefully—while Sera reached for her skirt. She didn't leave when Sera stood with the skirt in hand, covering her legs. Teresa waited until Sera crossed the floor with bare feet to accept the towel. Teresa took the moment to be her right, an Italian mother's right to check the goods in her son's best interests.

Only when Sera reached for the towel did the woman smile and disappear from the room. She vanished from Sera's sight as would a ghost, an image content and finally put to rest.

Neither had said a word.

*

Later, in the bathroom, Pep was dizzy and half aware of something wet on his chin but wasn't sure if it was spittle, lipstick or wine. In the end he just decided to ignore his chin rather than make too much fuss about his appearance. They were married already; what did it matter? She wasn't going anywhere.

He felt so comfortable not having to worry about the way he looked to her that he let the alcohol sway him pleasantly into the bedroom. Sitting on the floor, he took off his shoes and pants, leaving his shirt open and showing what he thought to be an impressive amount of chest hair, practically a goddamn sweater.

Bottle after bottle after bottle breathed, fell and died when fifty-seven of Pep's closest friends met for their wedding tribute dinner party. Married by proxy, they were actually man and wife some two months before, giving their vows over the telephone with Sera's brother standing in for Pep. But the matrimonial spirit of the party was not lost, it being Sera's first day in America with her new husband. Strangers, all of them, pushed back their chairs and raised their sloshing glasses in her honour. All of them except one.

There was a man named Sunderd who stood up from his table, stepped onto his chair and then the table, during the final round of *digestivi*. The other members from his table helped keep it from toppling over as he found his balance

over the empties and cautiously stood, straightening his
spine, lifting his head slowly and raising his glass precariously
far from his mouth.

Sentl, sentl, he said, until the room grew quiet. It seemed
the word 'listen' was the only Italian that he knew.

I want to tell you, he said in English, about this glass of
wine. About why we make toasts and clink glasses together.

Sunderd paused to sip from the glass. He was nervous
but suddenly enjoyed the eyes below him. He bent down and
picked up a bottle.

Do you know that a glass of wine is the best of man's
creations? To prove it to you I will show you how a man can
savour all of its qualities with each of his senses. He can raise
the glass to the light and see a wine's honesty. He can use
his nose and smell a wine's fragrance. He can sip from the
glass, juggling the juices between his cheeks to feel the wine
dance across his tongue. Swallow a sip and he can finally
taste the wine, the grapes, the earth itself. But the last and
most important thing the wine possesses is what it does for
the ears . . . when two glasses meet and ring in toast. And so,
my friends, let us push our glasses together in one final
wedding tribute:

> Here's to the girl in the little white shoes.
> She likes her liquor; she likes her booze.
> She lost her cherry but that's no sin,
> She still has the box the cherry came in!

With that, Sunderd finished his glass, tried to refill it with the
bottle in his hand and, finding it empty, proclaimed it another
dead soldier.

After a nervous pause, everyone, including Sera—to
prove she had a good sense of humour—laughed. But the
joke quietly burned inside her while the drinking continued.
Pep saw her cheeks were red, but didn't feel the heat.

More toasts to the new *moglie* proved just as ridiculous, Sunderd's setting the standard. Full bottles of water were used only to wash out a glass, toss the mixture on the floor as dishwater and ready the glass for something stronger, even more *vigoroso,* to help the groom.

The groom, however, was not helped so much. Hours later Pep seemed to straddle the bed, so high off the floor it felt like a billiard table. His feet caught in the blankets he tried to push away. Every movement made the bed swirl and engulf his limbs. When he pulled one leg out he lost a sock. Then, while he tried to brace himself to free the other foot, the first was again swallowed up by the bed's cover sheet. The more he struggled, the more the bed ensnared him, until finally everything but the mattress liner was kicked to the bottom of the bed, like a net that held his watch, a comb, one sock, his trousers and seventy-three cents in change.

Sera waited, now wearing her camisole, slip, stockings and a calm, vindicated smile. She waited for him to stabilize himself on the bed, stop shifting, retrieve a lost arm and adjust his knee to somewhere less hazardous. She waited for him to say something, give her some hint about what she should be doing with her hands, her mouth, but Pep seemed eager to do all of the work.

So she let him.

Sera lifted her arm when he had trouble grasping her breasts. She opened her legs slightly when his hand brushed her thigh, closed them again when he wanted her to shift a little from one side to the other. She even tried to catch his stabbing kisses, with her lips as puckered as she could make them, not because she wanted to be more responsive, but because she was afraid of him chipping her teeth with his. He jerked his head and body from side to side, knocking their noses together, fumbled to free the corner of his shirt, which was caught under Sera and somehow digging into his neck, and paused between kisses for a quick breath, sometimes two, only to shift again.

Nothing worked.

Finally he stopped, shifted and settled himself in the middle of the bed, his arms outstretched, to grip the sides and slow the swirling in his head. Sera was amazed at how calm she was. Yes, she felt responsible, but only because she'd let him drink so much. The thought that she was not attractive to Pep only entered her head for a moment when she noticed his little tent, in the very middle of the huge bed, getting smaller and threatening to topple over. But when Pep turned toward her, having found both his breath and his bearings, Sera pushed the thought away from her mind and looked into her husband's face. Still in one sock and blue boxers, not having the strength to raise more than an eyebrow, Pep was far from the man she imagined him to be. Instead, she felt sorry for him. He seemed so entirely out of his element.

Sera put him on his back in the mammoth bed and, resting an elbow on his chest, stroked his cheek, already growing the next day's stubble. His skin was smooth, oily and dark. He had blackheads on his nose. He had blackheads everywhere she looked. The pores on the backs of his arms and legs seemed full of coal, and she hardly had to squeeze the flesh in her fingers to watch the bits of blackness escape their tiny traps. She rolled his skin between her fingers, grabbing whatever she could stretch away from his ribcage, his collarbone, even his face, and flushed a foreign pinkness into his flesh, which was for a moment almost the colour of his nipples, but paler, like a dog's tongue.

Maybe she was thinking about a dog because of the way Pep was lying on the bed, his arms back, his stomach waiting to be scratched. But everything about him seemed to be waiting. Even the coal dust that she pinched out of him was slow to leave his pores.

When she decided to go beyond his skin and somehow feel his muscles, relaxed and stretched against his bones, she pressed down with her palms. His muscles didn't feel hard or strong, but their tightness impressed her. Pep was compact, not a tall man or particularly muscular, but a working man with long, dense muscles and huge joints. His body was economic, a pail filled with rocks and water. Not a part of him existed that wasn't created, shaped or callused by a shovel.

She saw that he didn't have a straight bone in his body. His neck, spine, nose, legs, even his arms warped at gentle angles, like dill pickles. When she uncurled one fist she found the result of some mine accident: the gnarled ends of fingers shot off at different angles, pointing everywhere at once. One finger was partially missing. He had an old man's hands, with wrinkles on his palms and strange blond hair popping out of his knuckles that she wished she could pluck. She fought an impulse to pinch and pull his skin taut in her hands. Above his knuckles the skin was grey, almost sun-spotted, but loose and amphibian—smoothed by labour instead of time. She couldn't imagine the skin ever breaking or changing colour. It was as lifeless as wrinkled rubber.

His whole body seemed at once smooth and polished by grainy oil and at the same time rough, beaten black by shovels and picks and falling rock. His fingernails had ridges on them like tiny washboards.

His legs were surprisingly hairless.

You have nicer legs than I do, Sera said quickly, as fast as she thought it. Pep winced and she stopped examining him by mashing her cheek into his nose. When she kissed him she pressed her face against his, forcing him to relax and not even use the muscles in his neck. When he pushed up his tongue she sucked on it and held it up with her teeth between breaths. And when she pulled his hand under her camisole to her left breast, choosing, proudly, the slightly bigger of the two for him to touch first, Pep's eyelids dropped almost immediately. They fell one by one, in time with the ending of a fairy tale he'd never even heard.

Don't worry, Sera said, surprising herself with words she thought she could never have said, I'll get you in the morning.

THREE

When will he get here?
I told you: in the morning.
But what time?

*

Later, not so many years later, she listened for his breathing to become regular, measured by a deep inhalation, a cool nasal spray of air on the back of her neck and a long—remarkably long—moment of silence before each new breath. After half an hour she slipped her hand out from under her pillow, pulled back her side of the blankets, quietly scissored her legs over the side of the bed and ended in a partial squat, eyes level with her husband's breathing, twitching face.

Pep was still sleeping soundly. His breathing was regular, methodical. She could imagine him working in the mine with the same rhythm. His lungs would keep time with the pick in his hand as if he needed the coal face to breathe. Though he was still young, only forty years old, the shadow that fell on his cheek made a labyrinth of lines across his face, spread out from the corners of his eyes like the belly of a leaf.

He wasn't handsome, even in his youth. His worst feature was a strong, almost straight Calabrian nose that gently curved to one side, unfortunately his left—the *sinistra*. The ends of his nostrils were bubbled now, and pushed straight out from the length of his nose, giving him the determined look of a man who could work, who could only work.

But he didn't dream, never could dream, never even jerked a leg or paw to chase a rabbit during a thousand and one nights of Sera's nocturnal sagas. The past lived in her dreams. Mediterranean people from other lifetimes—ghosts from her childhood—washed in and out of Sera's dreams like driftwood, moon-driven and faded with each night's tide, yet always recognizable to her mind's eye. They tumbled toward her, rolling like antique carpets, or simply appeared under her feet, warm, yielding and somehow expected.

Sera tripped over her father's body countless times; sometimes he got up and walked away without a word, and all that was left of him was a wayward string of lazy footprints in sand. Other times he just rolled over, cursed her for leaving the door open and chased some lizards out of the kitchen. She watched him grab for their tiny tails that broke off in his fingers and allowed their escape. She tried to tell him to stop, that the lizards were good luck, but the next second he and the lizards and the kitchen disappeared, and all that remained was a dull ache in her toe—where she'd kicked him—that ballooned into a throb until she woke up crying and holding either her foot, or Pep's. The people in her dreams never surprised or frightened her, no matter how quickly they emerged from the water, a shadow or another player's mask. Something always betrayed their presence, she thought, and allowed them to blend, to cocoon for a night's moment, beside whatever else she was thinking about. They were like a distant drum that eventually beat in time with her pulse, a drum that finally became her pulse.

Sera reached for her skirt and slippers. Instead of taking them out of the room to put on, she dressed in front of her husband's closed eyelids, tucking her flannel nightgown into her skirt and balancing herself with the back of a chair while she slipped on one slipper, then the other.

She would have worn running shoes if she had them, if anybody'd had them.

Then she put on a jacket, probably one of Pep's since it was handy, and, one resolute step after another, walked out of his dreamless life forever.

*

On another occasion Sera would have come back, Pep was sure of it. She would have left the house for only an hour, padded through coal dust to the tipple and back, maybe as far as the river or the side of the mountain to watch the clouds, back-lit and black in their centres, try to outmanoeuvre the moon.

She was given to those things. The night confided a sense of self that daylight could never articulate.

In the sun she could see and feel the air that usually blew coal dust into the corners of her eyes, invaded her pockets, lodged in the fabric of her coat or shot through button holes to rasp against her skin. On those days, when she came back to the shelter of her house, she rubbed the black specks of mountain out of her eyes with her palms and then ran to wash her face. If the wind wasn't harassing her senses, or clogging them with dirt, the air was so stagnant and porous, thick with heat, noise and summer smells, that she had little energy left to let her imagination stray. The effect was the same: during the day she felt rooted in the present.

But the night cleansed everything from the air, even the coal dust, and left her completely alone with her thoughts to stir their own smells. The night's air didn't crowd or fill her senses, but let her remember and imagine. By one of the river's smaller veins, Sera might have sat and watched stones ripple the water. She could see colours on the stones. Their backs were oil-stained and streamed slick against the moon-light. The night air was cool. She listened to the water swirling over and around the rocks and the distant chinkle of a mine horse climbing up a tunnel.

But the truth was that Pep couldn't figure out what she was doing there. She sat by the creek. She did that. Often. She was seen. But what did she see? What did she think? What did she remember? What was she hoping for? Did she know what would happen to her?

For all he knew she was snaring frogs, poking out their eyes and leaving them in bottles of rainwater to grow their 'third eyes'. Put one under your bed and, by approximation, gain the ability to read the future. They used to do that, superstitious people from the old country. But did she?

The night shift was just beginning its second hour, but without the coke ovens going, the mine seemed abandoned at the surface. They were deep in their tunnels, burrowing, leaving pillars, clearing rooms. They controlled the air and chipped away at what Pep called a gassy face. She imagined the layers upon layers of tunnels, the mountain becoming hollow as they tunnelled forward, then side to side, toward one another. When they retreated, they took what they could from the pillars and let the darkness crumble behind them. For them the weather was the same all year long: warm and wet and dark.

Pep used to describe the work to her before he changed to days. And Sera, in order to spend more time with him, stayed awake during the night, reading, walking or cooking, until he came home, ate his dinner and dragged his heels to bed. Most times he was too tired to even sort the blankets from the sheets, as if he'd lost his place in an old familiar book and could just as easily drop himself at the beginning or the last chapter as have to wonder about it. After washing the dishes Sera stored them away from the dust that settled over the kitchen, then crawled into bed with Pep.

They slept between different pages. Sera was always where she should be, underneath all of the sheets but one:

the sheet between her body and a bare mattress. Pep was one or two sheets above her. His skin didn't perceive the roughness of a blanket where he should have felt the smooth sides of cotton or flannel, and after a time Sera didn't bother to correct him. They slept from eleven in the morning until six in the evening, when Pep woke for supper and another night's work.

FOUR

Celi remembers the first time he was stuck in a mine and Pep
took him out. After most rumblings, the workers just packed
up and went home—those blasts, of course, where nobody
went missing. The explosive coal dust that hung in the
tunnel's air made further work too hazardous. But Pep heard
the rumbling that night, like a stomach's groan for food,
before anybody else. He leaned over to Celi, said, it's all over
for tonight, and started walking down the man-way toward
the main tunnel and out. There wasn't much cause to run, he
said, it wasn't a big rumbling, just enough to fill the mine with
dust for the rest of their shift, maybe into the start of the
morning shift. After fifteen years he could smell the difference: which rumblings to walk from, which to run from and
the others—the ones he thought about occasionally when he
heard thunder in the sky—when it didn't matter what he did
or where he ran. Partway down the slope Pep and Celi
stopped and waited in a cut-out the size of a closet for the
heaviest of the dust to die down. They waited far too long,
Celi thought, just for their eyes to adjust to the change of
seeing the world by inches instead of feet. They should be
running for the entrance. But Pep held tight, listening for
voices. Minutes blew by with the dust and finally Pep began
moving, walking slowly and calling to the others that he was
heading out. Yards later they met others. The pinpricks of
light that shot from their head-lamps drowned in the swirling
of smoky dust and didn't help much. Mostly Pep guided

himself and the younger miners by memory, it seemed, and by a slight breeze that blew particles of rock against his cheeks. He seemed to know that for fifty yards most of the dust would be coming straight at them, until they reached the main room where the connecting tunnel—the one that had blown—met up with theirs. We've got time, no need to get excited and lose yourself, he said out loud to the other miners. Grab a hold of your mate's belt. Walk when I walk. Pep's words reassured them. He talked to them matter-of-factly, as a radio announcer might give a weather forecast. And they believed him. He believed himself. After they rounded one side-tunnel, a heavier pelt of dust brushed past Celi's face. They knew they were out of the worst of it. The rest of the walk would be down, with the dust swirling at their backs, then an easy climb, on a thirty-degree pitch, straight out to cleaner and cleaner air, and finally outside to the night and the stars and the clear, white moon. (Slack rock, ten to twenty feet away from Celi, skips down the man-way.) A tag count showed thirty-five missing that time, but two of those men had got out of the mine and just kept on running. In the morning the fire boss said a good portion of the tunnel had caved, making for some extra labour for those who wanted it: stink work. A horse was missing too, one of the older pullers that was put into an unused shaft between loads. Probably dead, but the horse was pretty old so it was no great loss. The strange thing was that they found it about two weeks later, still alive, and carried it out of the mountain to daylight for the first time in God knows how long. The horses that work in the darkness of the mountain don't seem to miss the daylight, Celi thinks. Once they start working days, their eyes adjust to the mine's routines as quickly as their muscles do, dragging rail cars of coal up the pitch. Generally, three-horse spike teams, harnessed nose to tail, pull the cars up the slopes. The horses learn how to count the cars and refuse to pull more than six up the pitch. They know it's too heavy without even trying. A day's work is a day's work, sun or no sun, and then they're allowed to settle back into their stalls for night or day, depending on their shifts. A huge pail of water and a tub of oats is their pay. But that horse, the horse that lived, was named Charlie, Celi remembers. He'd survived by eating part of his wooden harness, gnawing on one of the two long poles that connected him to his cars. He drank water that seeped from the cap rock and dripped into shiny black pools. Fallen bits of coal and rock kept the invisible puddles from running down the tunnel's slight incline and disappearing into the rubble. Charlie was the only blast survivor ever to last seventeen days alone in a coal-mine. And as for Celi: he and another twenty-five miners brought the horse into the town pub to celebrate, a ritual that lasted barely two days. After three feeder buckets of oats and brandy on the second evening, the horse died, killed with kindness. An hour after that, so did the party. But the lessons Pep taught Celi that day stayed with him. If you want to get out of a mine safely, you stay calm; you stay put until you can see; and you learn from others. Pep learned these lessons the same way, Celi knows, from others like him. You don't last that long in the mine if you aren't sharp to what they're telling you. (Timbers, rubbing against the cap rock, screech and chirp beside him.) He should notice the tags, Celi says, sometime after seven. And to himself: that doesn't mean much unless we know what time it is now.

*

But she'd seen more:

Six rescue searchers carried the horse out of the coal-mine on a huge stretcher. Because the horse was thin and bony from starvation—it had been over two weeks—the miners each needed only one arm to support its weight. Their shoulders were level, as if the horse was not even heavy enough to imbalance their other, empty hands. And Pep was one of them. He walked carefully on the rock-littered ground, squinting as he came out of darkness.

Except for the search-lamps on their heads and the horse's black hoofs sticking out on one side, they looked like pall-bearers in their coal-blackened, matching uniforms. Their procession was slow, deliberate. Pep was one of the shortest men, in front, which made the stretcher slant, threatening to spill its rider. This also gave the crowd outside the mine a full view of the horse's head, neck and ribcage. The horse, looking calmly at all of the kneeling people, stretched its legs, took a large breath, and blinked.

The praying crowd outside travelled immediately from that afternoon back into morning. Time seemed to regress as their emotions reversed directions. Many of the women— including Sera—began again to cry and a few of the children followed their example. A small boy wearing lederhosen spoke the only intelligible words to a woman in a crumpled dress beside him: Look Mom. It's only a pony, that's all. It's just a horse.

#

News of the tapping noise behind the wall of rubble and coal spread through the town faster than the fire that had skipped along the top of the mine and caused the blast. A crowd gathered almost immediately outside the entrance to the mine-shaft beside the tipple. They waited for seventeen days.

Doc Sunderd heard them waiting. From inside the wash-house he listened to the men pounding tent-pegs into the ground, the women gathering their children for picnic dinners with neighbours. He thought he could even hear their clothes rasp, buttons against buttons, as they hugged one another and waited together. He could hear their knees bend and touch the ground and their hands come together in front of their faces. He listened to them shutting their eyelids. And he mouthed their silent prayers for the tapping noise to continue.

By the fourth evening Sunderd had prepared twenty-seven bodies to be examined by a coroner's jury of ten miners. Still other segmented bodies lingered in the wash-house sinks, waiting, just like the crowd outside, for news about the tapping. This was how Sunderd liked to think of them: lingering with hope. As he reconstructed and identified bodies, he had gradually begun to think of them as though they were only waiting to be put together, and enjoying the wait before they could be tagged, stamped and put back into the ground. The longer they listened to the tapping noise, thought Sunderd, the longer they lived in his wash-house.

Sunderd did not think, or tried not to think, about death. His was a creative act, and in his narrow creativity he found that he could avoid contemplating the destruction that gave him his job—at least until the tapping miners were freed. Until then, he and his bodies waited, hoping with the crowd outside that the tapping would not stop.

A half-bottle of scotch was his only helper. It was his friend who never left him, and he never left it. The bottle held his hand as he unwrapped, with the other hand, the bundles of men. He liked the touch of the bottle's cool, smooth glass. No matter how hot and fetid the air became, the bottle stayed composed, indifferent.

When the stench of damp coal and rotting wood was fanned out of the mine, sometimes the wind shifted in the direction of the wash-house. All Sunderd had to do was look at his friend, sloshing happily from within, to forget the smell. The liquid inside the bottle was the opposite of fire and explosions: it trickled and flowed naturally, according to gravity. Fire in a mine defied nature, burning methane gas along the ceiling until it came to a pocket of explosive coal dust. But watching the liquid in the bottle washed away the memory and smells of the dust within Sunderd, just as water had quenched the burning timbers within the mine.

Each time, after the searchers left the burlap bundles for Sunderd, he brought the bottle out of his pocket and shook it in front of his eyes. When the liquid settled and the bubbles disappeared, he made his other hand fold back the burlap. The last bunch came to him in a wheelbarrow, hidden underneath rubble and broken mining picks. The searchers had covered the bundles of hands, arms, feet and legs with debris from the mine so that they could slip them past the crowd waiting outside.

When the pieces of bodies began getting larger, Sunderd guessed that the searchers had finally dug beyond the origin of the blast. His work would soon be getting easier, he thought. After a few more constructions, the rest of the bodies would be either suffocated or dead by carbon-dioxide poisoning—'blackdamp' the miners called it.

For the most part, brass tags identified the torsos of the bodies. Before going into the mine, each miner was required to pick up an ID tag from the lamp-house, along with his head-lamp and mining equipment. There weren't many places to hide the tags. Because most of the miners wore only wool shirts and pants next to their bodies—to guard against staying wet for a whole shift—the tags were easy to find. Sometimes they were hidden behind the men's collarbones. It wasn't the first time Sunderd had had to pick something foreign from a man's skin: timber shavings, gunshot, sometimes a tooth after a bar-room brawl, even some feathers, once, from a man who'd been kicked out of bed while holding a nasty, home-made pillow.

Once he had identified a torso and stripped and washed the coal-blackened skin, he began matching limbs by muscle, hair, skin colour and texture comparison: the skin's text. Sunderd used his own common sense to decide whose head or arm belonged to whom. His sense of aesthetics guided him: similar burn marks, matching hand and foot size, a sprinkle of moles, anything peculiar to the torso he was working with.

The bodies were so scattered throughout the mine that it really didn't make much difference to Sunderd where the searchers said they found them. Before the explosion many of the miners had started to run out, or what they supposed was out. Most were found in other workers' tunnels. With the floor rumbling under their feet, Sunderd supposed, and the methane in their nostrils, a frenzy of panic would have added to their confusion. The heavage in the mine, he thought as he scrubbed a foot, would have raised the ground beneath their own feet. Gravity reversed, support timbers would splinter and crack. Flames racing along the gassy ceiling would light their faces for only a second. Then there would be darkness.

Sunderd dropped the foot into a sink beside him and fumbled in his smock for the bottle. His friend was clear; there was no darkness within. He could see through the bottle.

Everything was so clear, he thought. The stupid, stupid quest for progress. Coal. Big money. A dream as mangled as the minds and bodies that chased it. The whole coal industry was mangled, in his opinion, he told the bottle. Fire bosses were hired by mine owners to police the gas levels, but everyone wanted as much coal as they could find, as quickly as they could find it. The fire bosses tolerated a man who could work the gas, a miner who kept it swirling high on the face. They lowered their safety lamps to the floor when they checked on him and their lamp flames never found the gas, never burned bright, feeding on methane. Never betrayed the miner for his officially illegal activity.

To Sunderd's eye, a safety lamp looked like a rectangular cheese-grater. He'd peered into one or two of them, always amazed that fire couldn't move through wire gauze. The holes, he learned, were longer than they were wide. The fire could breathe, grow, but never escape. How else could a flame possibly help a man, except when it was safely trapped inside a metal box?

But the miners didn't debate such magic, not really. They got paid by the amount of coal they dug. So they used the dangerous gases to soften and bubble the coal out faster than by pick. Using, instead of avoiding, the gas. The mine owners knew all about it, not that they would ever admit to it, no miner would. Full steam ahead. Use the gas if you can bring out more coal. More gas, more coal. More coal, more money for you. More money for you, more promotions for me. Don't you have a son in Junior High, bring him down, I'll hire him. He can buck coal. You can leave the Crowsnest and go back to the old country a rich man. Full methane ahead!

Even the dinky-drivers got more money if they drove more coal out of the mine. And the coal-buckers too, pushing the coal down the chutes faster and faster until they fell into the chutes themselves, or got promoted. One or the other, up or down. After a blast in the mine, anybody left standing got a bonus, his pockets so full he couldn't walk.

But now they were praying for a different kind of pocket, thought Sunderd. Pockets of air in the mine for the tapping miners. Outside the wash-house he could hear the steady hum of the fan pushing clean air into the mine and drowning out the crowd's prayers. All coal-mining stopped when a man was missing, alive or dead. The coke ovens, the coal sorters, the rail cars: almost everything to do with the normal function of a mine was shut down and silent. If a fire was suspected they turned off the air pumps.

Once in a while Sunderd heard the shrill voices of children yelling, playing games to pass the time, and each time he smiled. They were lucky, he thought, to be too young to understand. They built sand castles out of river rocks and shale. Stories about the mine where timbers magically grew to touch the ceiling no matter how short they had been cut were just that: stories. Tall tales. Something to dream about instead of dreaming for. The miners dreamed the mine for money.

But during the tapping, the people came together and propped up each others' sagging shoulders. They did emotionally what Sunderd was doing physically: selflessly reconstructing other people. Sharing.

He heard them indulge each other with wonderful ideas: they're probably just sitting in there making up songs and tapping them out on that rail, or, he never could keep a decent beat. Listen to that racket! Sunderd could imagine their frantic hugs in his mind: they clung to each other for so long that under normal circumstances they would have been embarrassed. Their thoughtlessness for what they looked like—even though he could not really see them—made even the bottle he was holding warm with happiness. He caught himself wishing it would never end. That the tapping noise would go on forever.

The coal-black, clenched hand in Sunderd's hand stole the smile from his face as quickly as if it had reached up and pulled down the corners of his mouth. He did not let it drop, as he had the foot, but squeezed his bottle, feeling the security of its resistance to being squeezed. As with all the others, the hand's fingernails had ridges on the top, like the edge of a quarter. The nails flared back slightly at the ends, proving the man's lifetime of work with his fingers. As if he had been digging for fifty years to get a little money that always escaped his palms. His skin was thick and soft, with extra mounds of tissue on all of his knuckles, and the flat pads of his fingertips were especially suited for holding a shovel or pick. The hand had survived coal-mining for a long time.

The man Sunderd thought the hand belonged to was in pieces, looking very comfortable—for the first time in his life—lying in the bottom of a tub. He finally fit. If that wasn't really his hand or leg, he didn't complain. No explanation was necessary. In a way, the man was sharing himself with another man so completely that his kindness was beyond words. His silence was expected and deserved. He had given himself to another man and another man had given to him.

All this was nonsense, of course. Sunderd knew it. He heard the crowd's prayers stop and their cries begin. From a small window in the wash-house he saw the world teeter, ever so slightly, as soon as the casket-like horse was brought from the mine. The people hugged themselves—not others—and clasped their own faces, trying to catch their tears and somehow put them back where they came from.

Sunderd watched a mother push her son away, then grab for him. He had been tugging at her dress. She lifted her eyes from the gravel and said something so quietly to the boy that even Sunderd could not hear. The boy picked up a scooter, or a box—Sunderd couldn't see—and walked away.

A half-dozen people closest to the stretcher stared at the horse without moving even their chests to breathe. The horse returned their stare with one bulging eye. The other eye was against the stretcher and could not be seen, or see. Sunderd wondered if the horse could see at all so soon after leaving the mine. Some of them, he'd heard, went blind hauling cars through the mountain's darkness. Nobody found out until after the horses were put to pasture, or began working days.

The searchers laid the stretcher beside the tipple, twenty feet from Sunderd's wash-house. They did not go back into the mine. Common sense screamed to the crowd that if the only thing brought out of the mine was a rail horse, there was nothing left to hope for.

Sunderd's ears throbbed.

A woman wearing a bright yellow dress ran up to one of the searchers and struck him with an open palm.

Why did you bring this, this thing out? Why didn't you

help my husband? He's still tapping. Can't you hear him? He's still tapping. Isn't he? He is. I heard him.

When another woman (it was Sera) pulled her away from the searcher, he walked away, toward a barn connected to the tipple. His two-headed pick hung lifelessly in his right hand. His face was black, unrecognizable. Sunderd thought it was odd the way the pick did not even swing as the man walked. The women disappeared by the time Sunderd looked back for them. When he returned his eyes to find the searcher with the pick, he saw only the open door of the barn. It might as well be shut, he thought. A shadow blocked his vision of the barn's interior. The darkness was the barn's second door and made Sunderd wonder about the darkness inside a mine. There must be many second doors within a mountain. A world behind the world where a man or horse could be trapped and only heard.

But what good was speaking out anyhow? Who really heard anyone but themselves, except in times of hope? Sunderd, a doctor, knew this to be true. After the blast, the people outside the mine had listened. They had really listened to something else besides themselves. Sunderd knew they had. He'd heard them listening.

Now they only heard their own cries. Their hands were wet with tears. They didn't hear or see the searcher in the barn come out with a bucket in his hand. Sunderd was the only one, the only one who could see so clearly.

Everything in front of Sunderd was as transparent as the bottle he gripped inside his pocket. He could stand back, removed, and watch the people staring at the horse, the horse staring back at the people. He saw the oats inside the pail as the man brought it past him. He was the only one who was thinking about, watching and listening to something else besides himself. Even the searcher was involved in his own business. Sunderd, he knew, was alone.

They're drowned, said the searcher, putting down the bucket.

Sunderd didn't know who the man was talking to, until he looked Sunderd in the face, waiting for an answer. He didn't want to be part of the picture he was watching.

His glassy friend that he brought out of his pocket couldn't hide him. The man was still watching him.

Sunderd clasped the bottle harder and suddenly wanted to laugh at the liquid sloshing inside the glass. It was better to laugh with friends than at them, he thought. The bubbles popped in front of his face. The liquid settled.

He wondered how a man could drown inside a mountain.

Sunderd wished he had a mining pick or a knife to strike out at something. He forgot about the searcher, still watching him, and thought about the horse. He imagined he was the horse, within the mine after the blast, still tied to its mining cars. Ignorant of what had happened, like a child, yet pulling the chains of his wooden harness relentlessly. Tapping. Searching for some kind of direction, meaning. Without a harness he would be driven mad. He needed either resistance or ignorance just as badly as the crowd outside needed hope.

The resistance of the bottle in his hand no longer helped. He could never truly share himself with someone else. He was alone, just like the rest of the people outside the mine. He couldn't think. He couldn't speak. Fragments of ideas seemed to be falling all around him, trying to rise out of his mouth like the floor of a heaving mine. But what the hell did he want to say? What could he say—to that woman?

Was he listening to himself? Was that what you did in a mine: listen to yourself? He wanted to feel hope, either the crowd's hope or the horse's ignorance. He wanted to free himself from the bottle and his job and all the people around him. Watching him.

What is mine in the mine is yours, he said out loud to the

horse's bulging eye. As soon as he said the words, he regretted breaking his silence. His feet unsure of themselves, Sunderd wobbled toward the horse. His knees touched the ground. His hands rested on top of the horse's pail.

Through the bucket Sunderd left the crowd and watched the oats swirl with each puff of his deep breaths. He felt more comfortable the further he stuck his head into the darkness, until he could see nothing at all.

*

Inside the mine's night Celi speaks in whispers. He is cold, though their tunnel is warm enough. The mine is a constant forty-six degrees Fahrenheit every day of the year, something Pep liked to brag about occasionally: where else could you find work like that? *No where else in the world.* But it is their inactivity, Celi thinks, that makes the first chills begin to soak through his woollen shirt, shivers that slide along his skin and muscle to settle like dew, finally, next to his bones. They sit on the ground and listen to the timbers creaking between darkness and rock. Rocking noises saturate their mine-shaft. A timber's brace rubs against the cap rock above, sending low-pitched moans down the pole into the floor. The knots in the wood twist and chirp under the pressure. They are a ship's groans, lonely shudders that move and sink through wood: sad, distant and noxious. As if from the sea. No sense moving about, Celi says, as much for his own ears as for Fina's. No sense at all. The guys Pep sends will just find us later than they should have, both of us lying in different shafts with broken legs. (Silence.) Sorry, he says. Best just to sit tight. *Sit tight,* Fina repeats. They are quiet for a long while before either speaks again, until the timbers prompt Fina to ask Celi the same question as before: *But what should we do?* Quietly this time, trying to impress on Fina some added meaning, Celi says the only word he can without yelling at him: Wait. (Again: silence.) *Hey, do you hear that?* It's the timbers creaking. Just the timbers. *Those aren't timbers; those are birds. Listen. Can you hear that? That sound: those are birds, aren't they?* It's nothing but timber noise. They don't bring canaries into the mine any more. It's the wood. *No, listen.* It's the wood. Not birds, not miners, I'm telling you. Listen to it for God's sake! (Another long moment drifts through the tunnel between them.) After that the words they speak come in sputters and gulps. There is no vote taken, no question asked. Fina, who starts talking first, seems just as eager to fill the tunnel with words, any words, as Celi wants to listen to a story drained from darkness.

*

The Calabresi say that a baker's apprentice—just a boy—invented tortellini soon after he fell in love with his boss's wife, a Bagnarota. The apprentice was making spaghetti, stringing long green threads all over the kitchen, drying it on the backs of chairs and across counter tops, hanging it over mug racks and pipes with lines tied from one end of the room to the other, when he saw her for the first time.

He'd made the pasta from twenty great flour mounds, capped with fresh eggs and minced spinach. He'd folded, stretched, folded, stretched and finally cut the green dough into long strands as fine as hair. *Spaghettini* they called it, tenuous spaghetti, strung across the room like seaweed, to be eaten, the next day, with a sauce made from octopus dye. Flour sprinkles kept the pasta from sticking to the lines and chairs, but dulled the spinach and gave the room a hazy stillness. The moisture evaporating from the dough made the air cool and damp. And he watched the woman between those green strands, as she moved back and forth, checking his work.

The pasta, she was thinking, must stay pliant, even while

it dried. The sauce depended on it, no matter what the dish: *cappelletti* hats, *fettuccini* ribbons, *gemelli* twins, *linguine* tongues, *orecchioni* ears, priest's hats, trout's eyes or *tagliatelle* nests. She needed just the right texture to catch the black granules in the octopus dye and make her guests devour their plates with twirling fingers and open, black lips.

The Bagnarota was so intent on her work that she didn't even notice the boy was there, in the kitchen, sitting on one of her husband's chairs. He was covered in flour and spinach and almost dressed in spaghettini, like a fisherman caught and reeled in by his own net. Or he might have been part of the net, actually made from pasta, knotted by currents, stretched and spun and drying himself on the sand beside an equally silent jellyfish.

When she seemed satisfied with the spaghettini, he watched the lines in her face relax and make her eyes grow softer, larger somehow. They were brown eyes, brown puddles that he followed and pored over with his own. He imagined his nose sinking into them, into their dampness, and disappearing—just the tip—as he kissed her lips. Watching between the pasta vines, catching sight of her between the strands without turning his neck, he could see those two brown pools more clearly than anything else in his life. Her eyes didn't dart or shift from one place to another. They lingered and swept, drained and puddled again. When she began to finger the strands more gingerly he could see she was simply enjoying the coolness on her skin and nails. Her eyes grew wide and told him she was smiling.

She left a finger's impression, her thumb print, flattened in one hair and perceptible to no one—she thought—except herself. She liked that, he knew. She simply liked the touch of pasta, which was something far more important than guessing how many times it had been stretched. Her husband would do that, of course, without fail, without error. At a moment's glance the cook would know precisely how many strands of fettuccini had passed over the *chitarra*—a wooden guitar that is played only in Abruzzi kitchens, with strings of pasta. Rolling the dough across the instrument garnered uniformly sized noodles, but it left nothing for a boy's imagination.

Thankfully, the Bagnarota left before seeing him for who he really was: a poor apprentice, feigning sleep (possibly) and covered in as much spaghettini as he had made.

Her eyes—those two brown puddles—haunted him. He wanted not only his nose to disappear when he kissed her, but his whole face right after his nose, as she saw him, and then his whole body, swallowed up in her eyes, slipping down, down, his legs disappearing, ankles, toes and all, as she loved him, too, for the first time.

But he knew she never would. She was married. He was nothing. He was less than nothing: a stupid, dream-struck boy who made green spaghetti.

That night, and for three more nights, he couldn't help going to her house. Each time he saw his boss, the cook, close the curtains and turn out the lights in their bedroom. At best he saw a shadow, a silhouette, that vaguely resembled hers. But the outline reminded the apprentice of watching her in a kitchen lined with pasta, so he was able to leave with his smile intact. On the fourth night he was lucky. The cook was out, playing cards, or maybe watching somebody else's window; the details didn't matter to the apprentice. What mattered was finally being able to see the cook's wife and let his eyes swim in more secret waters than her eyes.

She was already asleep by the time he got to the house. Her husband out, she'd gone to bed early, and all the apprentice could see—squinting, through the iron bars outside her window—were the strewn edges of her sheets and a minute corner of flesh where one sheet ended and another began. That small stretch of skin was her navel.

The next morning, in his kitchen, the apprentice made

the first tortellini. He fashioned the pasta exactly like the Bagnarota's navel: small, twisted donuts without centres, which he filled with the most delicate, most expensive meat he could find: minced veal.

When the apprentice finished his creation, the cook, upon recognizing the navel, drowned the boy in his largest pot. And that is why green tortellini—the colour of jealousy—is best served hot and spicy, submerged in a pale, translucent broth.

*

The afternoon the horse was found, Sera walked home alone, without waiting for Pep to change or wash. She didn't know that there wasn't a place for him to clean himself. Sunderd's bodies had taken over the wash-house so Pep would be washing at home, as he had for the past two weeks, just as soon as his pick, shovel, hat and lantern were hung to rest. She'd hardly noticed the change in his routine during the search for the missing miners. The days were blurred by tears and tapping sounds, hope and rumour, anything that dripped or ticked like a watch, anything that could be expected to fall, trickle or seep from hidden corners, hidden eyes and hidden mouths.

Now the days, weeks and months would begin again to gush. It was always easier, she knew, to look back and remember than it was to look forward, to wait for something. The mourning could begin now, finally, and then fade.

Sera left the mine site without giving the horse and the doctor another thought. Sunderd, at that time, was only one poor man among many. She walked slowly on the dirt path, more slowly than usual, straying from one side to the other to kick a stone or a leave a footprint on a vacant spot that had been forgotten. The mine was only two miles from town and she might have decided to walk further, but her bleeding wasn't quite over. Bears could smell the blood, menstrual or not, Pep had told her. Long walks weren't smart.

Despite Pep's advice, Sera took her time. She had little faith in men's stories and even less in their cautionary tales. She decided she would have her picture taken with the horse, for luck perhaps, the next day, after the mass burial. Again miners would strip the earth, scraping layer after layer from the black soil until they reached approximately six feet down, fourteen feet wide and twenty-three feet long. Crosses and bits of broken marble would litter the huge grave, where it would remain, for years, bloated and dark. A small, impossibly white picket fence, not tall enough to confine a rabbit, would surround the group, with a little memorial sign to mark their lives digging into this earth. It had happened before. She knew the routine.

What wasn't so usual was how she felt at that moment. The images she'd seen earlier in the day seemed to be following her, or at least made her start to walk a little faster. She saw the horse, and Pep. She saw the woman strike Pep across the face. And for an instant she thought she herself had struck him, just in those seconds when she was running toward him.

Instead Sera reached for the woman, helping her back to her people. Sera put her arm around the woman's waist, but felt the woman carrying her more than anything else.

Walking by those images, kicking stones and weaving around those thoughts that sprang to mind, Sera felt as tired and alone as she had outside of the mine. Moments like that, when Pep was sleeping, or working, or just his quiet self and *breathing*, made her wish for Italy. Italy seeped into Sera's present. She could imagine the Mediterranean washing away the Crowsnest and her life there, and when she gave in to those thoughts her wishes broke free, flooding her dreams. She talked with her dead father, with her friends and family who rolled toward her at night and rolled away by daybreak.

She felt the shadows of her past floating through her and over her like a cloud's gentle, cool eclipse of the sun. And in this way she could escape the weak Canadian sun, its frail eye, escape the dust. She could almost escape the Crowsnest.

And while she dreamed those dreams she kicked and thrashed her husband; she pushed him away with a knee, a toe, sometimes both feet, and drew him back just as quickly as she embraced her night's thoughts. She hugged Pep fiercely. She gripped his head, his ears. She threw a heavy thigh over his little body and pinned him to the mattress. She curved his body from one angle to another by digging into his spine with a well-placed elbow. From her dream world she asked him a thousand questions he could never answer and—as if in response to his muffled *whaaaa?*—she rolled away, taking his blankets with her. By morning she had twisted the blankets around their bed so completely that they ended up exactly backwards and inside out from where they'd begun.

For Pep's part, he thought only that she would have made a fantastic acrobat. With a row of chairs by their bed they could have charged admission. Sera, twisting, turning, flinging herself through the night, could then wake up to a fresh day, her night's work finished: that was the worst he ever thought of the matter. If he didn't sleep right through Sera's tempests, he usually forgot them by morning.

But in those dreams Sera invited Italy, her family, her past, into the real world of the Crowsnest Pass. The images trickled into reality, slowly at first, into greater and greater levels of daylight. Some mornings Sera could see water spreading thin across the moon in her window, and then, once those thoughts were let in at progressively later hours of the day, she saw those same things—the moon, the tide—rush toward her, around her and past her, like a boat swallowed in the Strait of Messina.

When she turned her head to look for them they might

be gone, but at least their memory seemed closer.
She'd wanted to hit Pep too.

*

Noon: the last shift of his first week was over. Pep walked
up the slope and toward the entrance behind the older
miners, two of his steps for every one of theirs. It took them
almost an hour of unpaid travelling time to get out. There
were hooks just inside the mine entrance where they snatched
their jackets before leaving the tunnel. And it was cold
outside, not at all like the mine.

The men were talking about how much they'd hauled,
who was filling more cars or who had his thumbs up his butt
and was probably planted by the mine bosses to lower their
quotas. Somebody else they knew just got 'promoted' to
night shift—poor bastard—so the pit boss could put horns on
him at a better hour. That was old news, it seemed to Pep,
watching their heads nod in the half-light; most everyone in
town had seen the fancy car parked outside the miner's house
while the *cornuto* worked. Stupid bastard probably knows,
said one of the miners, but likes his job too much to do
anything about it.

Pep was minding his own business. He wasn't comfortable yet and tried to blend in with the steady progression of
shadows and chalk-white eyes moving out toward the
wooden shack. If one man lost a wife while mining for coal,
then another lost a hand between rail cars, or a house in a card
game when he pissed away all his earnings.

As he walked, Pep clenched his hands and tried to crack
the black smears of coal and dirt on his palms, but they were
too greasy. He could see the lines on his knuckles but the coal
was worked too deeply into his skin for him to splinter the
darkness. He always stayed slightly on the outskirts of
motion, in and out of the mine, but once they entered the

wash-house he joined the frenzy of movement to get out of wet clothes.

The men wore woollen BVDs under their pit clothes, but Pep's skin wasn't used to the rough underwear yet. It itched and scraped him, wet or dry. If that in itself wasn't humiliating, most of their clothes were left in lockers that were almost bigger than he was. The doors were holed to let the air in and dry the muck off their clothes for tomorrow's shift. Those men who didn't use lockers left their blackened gear on giant meat hooks that hung from the ceiling. Pep didn't know why, didn't want to ask.

The lessons came inevitably, shift after shift. That day he'd learned about the heavage in a mine. When a timber was cut too short the pit boss had sent Pep to one end and another bucker to the other end. The log needed to be high enough to touch the ceiling, a difference of just over two feet.

Pep had seen the gap. The space between the log and the ceiling was real.

And yet they spent nearly an hour in an impossible tug-of-war, trying to stretch the log. Even though it was too heavy for the boys to lift, and at least two feet in circumference, they managed to teeter it on a wooden wedge, straddle and grip the ends with squatting bear hugs. Both their hats kept slipping off and rolling next to the checkboards, but Pep didn't care. The miners were yelling encouragement, more than he had ever heard.

Keep it up! Pull, pull, pull. We need that log to kiss the roof. You can do it!

Usually they ignored him, but every man who passed their room had said something. Suddenly he felt part of a team. He felt liked. If he felt foolish pulling on a tree trunk wider than his own chest, it didn't last. Every one of them seemed to want the log to grow. Every one of them thought it was possible.

Fifty minutes later, Pep's back, legs, even feet were wet

with sweat and mine water. He and his fellow log-stretcher were pushed aside as three timbermen lifted and then pushed up one end of the pole. Another man hunched next to the floor and steadied the base. When they had the pole standing almost upright, Pep aimed his head-lamp at the cap rock and watched the timber glide smoothly against the ceiling.

It was an hour later, on his lunch break, a tin box and half a prosciutto sandwich balanced on his knees, when they told Pep the floor had risen. He learned that the floor swells up in a mountain mine like bread dough, that it heaves and pushes base rock toward the ceiling, and he felt the food in his stomach harden into a flat, dark ball.

In the wash-house he moved slowly, taking off his shirt and pants as if he had the rest of the day to get clean. But when there was an empty spot beneath a shower-head Pep moved quickly under it. He didn't want to ask any of the men to reach the nozzle for him; none of the other buckers did. They'd all heard about the pole trick and were keeping to themselves, Pep saw. The water was cold but the buckers seemed to get out even faster today, before they were noticed or singled out.

Pep turned from the shower and started for the door. He walked carefully on the wet tiles, but obviously not fast enough.

You, what's your name?

Pep didn't look.

Hey!

He swivelled around too quickly, his feet slippery and aiding his spin. Pep was off balance but squarely met the eyes of a man working the black off his neck and chest with a dirty rag. The man, older than the rest of the miners, was standing slightly away from the shower spray and soaping himself into a muddy ghost that dripped grey bubbles.

Pep Rogolino.

You're one of them timber-packers aren't you?

The man was smiling soap across his face, but not unkindly, Pep thought. He took Pep's silence as the answer to his question.

Listen, you don't worry about that pole-stretching nonsense. There's something more important I want to tell you about. You're gonna think this is complete malarkey but I'll tell you anyway. See that little thing dangling between your legs? That thing there is going to get you in more trouble than anything else you'll ever own.

Black bubbled laughs all around.

Pep turned and left the showers, believing, just as the man had predicted, that the words were complete bullshit.

FIVE

Three words sliver through darkness toward Celi: *what about Sera?* The voice is high, practically running along the ceiling. What about her? *How did he meet her?* Why do you want to talk about that? *It's just a question to pass the time. Did you know her?* Yeah, says Celi. I knew her. Not too well mind you, but I knew her. She didn't grow up here so she wasn't too well known. She came from some hole-in-the-wall, in Calabria. A place called Scilla, not that it matters much. They're all the same down there. Celi knows the questions are worth answering just to forget the timber noises, but he's growing tired. He thinks about whistling to pass the moment and escape Fina's questions, but he knows he never would. No miner whistles underground. You don't do that, Pep told Celi, when he first started. Pep never told him why, but he sounded too serious for Celi to ask about it twice. Later, Celi figured out the superstition for himself. He heard an old timer singing on his way up the mine-shaft:

> *Avevo una casetta piccolina in Canadà,*
> *Un vasca con i pesciolini, un giardino pieno di lillà.*
> *E tutte le ragazze che passavanno di qua*
> *Dicevano che bella casetta in Canadà!*

A younger bucker started whistling beside the man, and Celi heard a smack and almost tripped over the boy's rolling body. We aren't out yet, said the old miner. Wait till we're out before

you start calling the roof to fall on our heads. Underground,
Celi learned, miners only sing or talk. Even the driver boys
have their ditties:

> My sweetheart's the mule in the mines;
> I drive her without any lines.
> On the bumper I sit, and I chew and I spit
> All over my sweetheart's behind.

Most of the songs Celi knows are worse than that one, but
every miner hears them, especially around lunch-time. It
takes too long to walk down the slope and eat outside, so they
sit and eat in their tunnels, listening to songs about crooked
bosses and miner's lifeguards:

> Miner's life is like a sailor's
> 'Board a ship to cross the wave. . . .

But Celi doesn't feeling like singing. The noises in their tunnel
keep his mind too heavy with thoughts for the lightness of
music. *I know about Scilla*, says Fina, interrupting a timber's
screech. *I've heard of it*. I'm tired, answers Celi. My throat's
sore from talking about Pep. All we gotta do is wait, you
know. Lots of guys have to wait out a shift in the dark. Most
of them are alone, too. They got nobody with them but
timbers.

*

Sera remembered the sea, the sea's smell, the sea like a living,
breathing creature, tethered only by the moon. She remembered fishermen dragging their tiny boats up to their door-
steps. Street labyrinths protected their boats from storms and
winds, making their city's blueprint layered, the inner confines as impenetrable to the sea as a huge man-made shell.

The houses followed the landscape, bending in gentle lines around their nearby hills like waves of stairs. Each town was structured next to the sea, designed to resist the sea, yet still able to embrace it with outstretched arms.

Sera remembered the houses. She saw their motley colours, picked out the ones she knew, as a fisherman might from his boat. The buildings were wedged together, yet every house was a slightly different shade from its neighbour. A dull pastel of distance, somewhere between terra-cotta and rusted peach, could be seen better from the sea than with a closer, more discerning eye.

In Scilla, Sera's town, the houses were more like bridges than buildings, built next to the sea. Every house along the water's edge had a tunnel built through its walls, just large enough to drag a row-boat under the kitchen floor. There were small stretches of rocky beach near the ends of the town, but they were seldom used. The tunnels were more convenient and the land pushed the houses too close to the Mediterranean for the *cittadina* not to love it a little. Some claimed to live their entire lives with one foot in the sea. At high tide, waves lashed at their walls, washed into their side streets and spread blue from their windows across the strait to Sicily. Sera could hear it lapping under her bed as she slept.

The tunnels let the town inhabit the Strait of Messina more than the rocky land allowed. And their boats were safe. The sea was kept out, blocked for the most part by the bulk of their walls, their rows of holed houses and the steep incline of the land. And in the afternoon, in the inner streets, fishermen rode fixed bicycles without wheels to pull their boats from the water. Long, taut ropes reeled their boats through the tunnels up to their bicycles. The fishermen pedalled, pedalling steadily after a full morning's work, pedalling their row-boats through the sand and cleaving a line from the water's edge through their tunnels. The boats disappeared under the house-bridges, sometimes under two sets of house-bridges, then reappeared, red, green, and dripping in one street or another. After they disconnected the lines from their bicycles' pulleys, the fishermen left the rowboats leaning beside their front doors.

The fishermen from Bagnara, just to the north, fastened their boats above the sea, using winches to raise them onto a storm wall. The wall curved slightly with the coast, stretching out like a porch to the strait and the very tip of Sicily. Besides the storm wall, there was nothing exceptional about Bagnara. It could be moved to any number of Mediterranean notches in the earth, any place choked between a hillside and the sea, any smudge of land with the sea rolling out like a long, blue page on its clearest days, a savage flapping rag on its darkest.

And yet again, there was one thing that made Bagnara peculiar, one single falsehood that left a sprawling, muddy truth: the women, it was rumoured, did all of the work. Their husbands were only seen playing card games in the afternoon, while the women of Bagnara came and went through fish markets, tended olive groves and picked bergamots. What the rest of Calabria didn't know was that the Bagnara women woke their husbands so early that the men could row out to sea, haul their nets and come back to their dreams before sunrise. Nobody saw them before two in the afternoon. It was the women, therefore, who moved through the usual course of daily events, through countless other rumours and countless other stories told, it seemed, on pages as long as the sea itself.

Every fisherman from neighbouring towns dreamed— only within the protection of a joke—of retiring to Bagnara, a town where the women were strong and mythic. They were called the Bagnarote, prideful women who some said could shed a man's misfortune as if they were burning a stained coat right off his back. They could burn the coat, they could simply take it off or they could sew him another. Their lives were woven in rumour and superstition.

Everyone in Calabria knew the proverb *If you are unlucky you must go to Bagnara.* There, the women could read the swirls of a man's future by spilling olive oil into pots of boiled water. The Bagnarote then cleansed him of his unlucky past by laying him out on his back, squatting over him and urinating. After that, nothing bad would ever happen to him, or, as some said, nothing worse. Their sea would be as calm as oil.

The women could erase seven years' misfortune from a shattered mirror as easily as throwing the shards over their shoulders into the sea. Some people believed that was what they did with both broken mirrors and discarded lovers: they multiplied a man's image by bearing him children, then they drowned him in sorrows. They could take care of a man and protect him from the sea or they could deliver him to the sea. Some said they married one man and bore the children of another. Yet, in their own way, the Bagnarote were never unfaithful. They were believed to be the most steadfast of wives. If crossed or angered they could run up one side of a man and down the other as though his head and shoulders were three soft, mushy stairs. They kept a man from other women the same way. If they swept his shoes with a broom, he would never marry. If they turned over a fish as they ate, his boat would capsize.

Inevitably, there were warnings, even nursery rhymes, that Calabresi mothers sang to their sons. No, they said, you don't want to meet a girl from Bagnara. She is not for you. You cannot win. You cannot be the master in your house. The Bagnarote are the true peasants; their station is fixed and you cannot lower them down.

But the sons did fall in love. They fell in droves when they caught sight of the young Bagnarote, partly from the stories about them and partly from the mystery unanswered in the stories. Sera too fell in love with the myths that grew

out of Bagnara, or the myths that she found in her night's
dreams. She thought about them often: the Bagnarote were
intelligenti like the fox, with brains like a good *cocuzza*, or
pumpkin. They were sensual and strong-willed, as *forte* as
pecorino sheep's cheese. They knew how to look into a man,
how to trick him or kill him with an evil eye, the man left
standing still, a spoon raised to his open lips. They hid their
revenge for years until it was as cold as the kitchen tiles in
Scilla. When he was least prepared, everything in his world
would crumble beneath him. Vengeance, they said, is always
a dish best served cold. They were devoted wives and yet
dependent on no one, independent of all. They went
wherever they pleased, crossed villages and travelled dis-
tances for their husbands, slipping through places that even
gypsies or vagabonds would not chance.

During the First World War it was the Bagnarote who
figured out how to steal bags of untaxed salt across the strait
from Sicily to Calabria. They began wearing layers of
clothing, always seven skirts, one on top of the other, and
hiding the salt next to their legs. They shrieked, screamed,
cried for their virtue, for the King of Italy, for the Blessed
Madonna, for Saint Vitus to save them from rabid dogs, for
Saint Spiridon to deliver them from evil thievery, for Saint
Lucy, protectress of breasts, for the Four Horses of the
Apocalypse to run around the world, all this and more, if an
Italian soldier so much as pointed to their bulging hips. Then
they stepped off the pier and walked from Reggio di Calabria
through Villa San Giovanni through Scilla, all the way to
Bagnara, selling the salt in black markets along the way.

It was the salt that made their hips sway like cleavers,
little bags that would be warm and more precious for where
they came from than for what they held. Despite the extra
weight, or more likely because of it, the women of Bagnara
had the most elegant gait in all of Italy. Even in Sera's day,
decades later, even in summer, the Bagnarote wore seven

skirts. The outermost skirt was black but the rest were different colours, and nobody, including Sera, knew what each one meant.

There were a thousand such towns that she remembered during her Crowsnest walks. Bagnara was just one, Scilla another, and Sera knew she had abandoned them all. Italy was as full of seaside towns as America was of promises. And she'd listened to those promises, it seemed, from the sea's pages, from the sea's lying tongue itself.

Yelping like Scylla's barking bay, enticing her to cross the Mediterranean, to leave her home, the sea brought Pep's letters and with them the images and smells of America. Pep, too, was just one of those images from those letters from America. From the first line in his address to the last, the words she'd burnt that day seemed as much from America as they did from him.

*

Pep walked away from his house, carrying the grip in his right hand. He liked leaving early in the morning, especially the days when it was so early that he could just beat the rising sun and see the moon in the same sky. On those days the moon was usually a dim sickle or a sliver, the colour and size of his nail's quick, in navy blue. But he hardly noticed these things; what he liked about this time was his solitude. Nobody, except the moon, saw him.

Sera once called the moon a thief, like the peasant labourer who steals baskets of olives—even the land—from the sun, who owns them. The day's eye, she said, reminding him. Do you remember that?

He did and he didn't.

Today, he walked away from the memory.

He was quickly out of Dagotown and turned right at the corner of Main Street, pointing himself toward downtown and walking quietly along the side of the road. The Black Nugget Café was open early enough for him to stop for coffee. And within ten minutes he was there, the first customer before the Millionaire Club arrived, a group of old farts who solved the world's problems by nine and left for the barber-shop rich with schemes by noon.

If he hadn't decided to work the four more years beyond his miner's pension, he might have been stuck with those gossip-mongers. But he'd stayed. After the dust became too much for his lungs, Pep had taken a job outside the mine.

When I left the mine face, he said out loud, they had to hire three guys to do my work.

After that, he pinched empty cars to the tipple, using a lever on one to push seven or eight up the rails and back up to the screens.

Evidently this was something that only the strongest men could do by themselves. The finger that he waved in front of the waitress seemed to change his words into more of a challenge, a record to be beaten, than the story of his life. She wiped the dust off the counters with a damp cloth, without shifting the small racks of packaged jam and honey or the salt and pepper shakers.

You gotta have the wind, mind you. If you don't have the wind you're not gonna do it. Even if you pinch four cars you can't stop. You have to go back and restart the whole mess again, take less. No sirree, you can't do it.

These were old stories, long dead yet never buried. He liked to resurrect them, take them out to the town bars and give them exercise. This was what usually happened: whoever was sitting at the next table heard how he caught his hand between two cars and smashed his fingers, how he walked alone two miles into town and how he kept the glove on so that most of his fingers wouldn't come off with it.

Then Pep laughed, uncurled his fist to show the lines of proof: smooth visible scars, a bad setting, two missing nails and a digit missing from his pinky.

See these hands? These are working man's hands.

The person, whoever he was, said nothing, nodded to Pep and caught a sympathetic wink from the waitress.

Today it was the waitress herself who did the nodding, without anybody else in the café to wink at.

At what point Pep became old, at what age his listeners became the men at other tables, was impossible to know. They started listening to him simply because he was that old bugger with a story he needed to tell, more for himself than for his listeners. He may have reached that point years ago, years before he actually became an old man, even before Sera left him. One could even add *so she left him* or, just as likely, *because she left him.* It could have been either one.

The change alone was interesting. He used to gamble; the money slipped away, stayed away. So he stopped. He had youth, a marriage. Everything ends. Everything's fertilizer: Pep was the first one to admit that. From shovels and picks, he now clenched his hands around coffee cups and beer chasers. He worked a ten-hour late shift for fifteen years, never missed a night; now he counted tags and lamps. After every pay cut or lapse in safety he told the mine bosses they could kiss his Royal Canadian Ass, grabbed his belt buckle to prove it and still got rehired in the morning. Now he just worked mornings. He was never sick, never cold, and his weight hadn't changed from a trim hundred and forty-five pounds since he was twenty-one. His knobby wrists and barrel chest proved he was a worker, a man made for work, even if he was old and did meagre jobs to keep himself busy. But he never missed a shift in his life.

*

He's coming. He'll be here soon.

＊

The afternoon Sera came home from the mine rescue, she brought her day's visions with her. Hardly talking to Pep, she was still shaken by the idea of hitting him, not that she thought his skin would feel the sting that would make her palm burn.

She went about the kitchen, making him his supper, suddenly tired of his routines, the way he came home from the mine and ate a self-made stew of whatever was around, no matter what she put in front of him. He mixed it all up in a bowl, whether it was hamburger and spuds or eggs and toast. His breakfast stew of shredded bread squares sopped up the yolk in his bowl until he added grape jelly to turn the whole mess green. Green eggs.

That was the only time of the day Pep smiled. He might have felt like a painter, Sera thought, mixing just the right compounds for his stomach's canvas, but she doubted it. While the Bagnarote always left a little food on their plates, so they would return some day to finish it, Pep couldn't see that far past the tines of his fork. The man worked, drank, ate and slept. It seemed enough for him. The Pass was enough for him.

Sera wanted to do more than dream at night. She wanted to give her days more colour than the black and white memories from her past. Everything in the Crowsnest seemed to her so terribly black and white, with varied levels of dusty grey. And all so they could go back to Italy with more money than they'd ever known; it was a fantasy she'd long since abandoned. Instead, she grasped for other dreams.

Most days she doubted they would ever leave.

Most nights she woke amazed she was still here. It seemed every night she stole the blankets from Pep and dreamed them back from the black market by morning. His blankets would spread across Italy, warming a hundred other toes, before Pep ever woke to notice they were missing. In the morning they were back again, so what did it matter?

She never told him where she'd been to buy them back. He wouldn't have understood the smallest feather of a dream, let alone a whole pillow's worth of real flight. And he wouldn't have known how to find a dream as one would a scar, a path or channel in one's skin, or how to leave a dream and have to walk back. *How does anyone learn these things, except by themselves?*

So that evening, as usual, Sera stole the covers from Pep's side of the bed. She didn't even wait for sleep before taking them. Seeing the horse brought out of the mine made her night more fitful, harder to find. When she was finally asleep, two hours later, she prodded him in the buttocks with her left big toe.

There's somebody knocking at the door, she mumbled. Go see who it is.

Every night that she was angry with the Pass, Sera's dreams washed it away. Outside, thirty years before that night, a wedge of limestone one thousand, three hundred feet high, four thousand feet wide and five hundred feet thick was falling—no, sliding—down Turtle Mountain's face, crumbling, rolling, skipping off the mountain's base and cartwheeling its fragments down empty streets, crashing through kitchens and living rooms, right through paintings, walls, and out again to back yards, trampling every fence and outhouse into a stockpile of toothpicks. Pep's house fared better, being in the furthest corner of the town and at the edge of Sera's dream, but the houses nearest the rock face were the hardest hit. The rolling boulders—huge rock marbles, really—obliterated the ground floors and carried both the second floors and their occupants away, riding on the tops of those spinning rocks, like sleeping clowns on unicycles.

At four hours after midnight, April 29, 1903, many of them were, on the town's most remembered night in history, still asleep.

Their top floors teetered, swivelled twice and just plain rolled away. Some of them went to bed near Turtle Mountain's base and woke up on the other side of the bed on the other side of the room at the other side of town with a marvellous view of Bluff Mountain and a dusty pile of rocks.

The rocks travelled so far that people claimed they rode on a cushion of air. But Mines Inspector William Pearce later said: The best explanation of how the slide acted is to take a pack of cards and throw them away from you. You will find that the top cards go the furthest.

In Sera's dream, as in most dreams, the deck was stacked. And because of that, Pep fared better than he would have if he'd actually been in the slide. Most of the miners said that, when it came to mine blasts, Pep had horseshoes up his ass every time.

But the unluckiest thing that Pep ever did in his whole life, the unluckiest thing that anyone could have done in any life, when his one-storey house threatened to float away on those rocks, when the rocks loosened the house's foundation and his wife was prodding him now with both big toes to get up and answer the door, and the rocks were rolling right through his kitchen, past the sitting room, through his bedroom, probably right under the bed and out again, with toe-nails prying into his spine and rocks rolling through the front yard and over that green patch on their lawn, the worst thing he could have done was roll over on his stomach and cover his ass with a pillow.

*

Dreams are borne on pillows. Each pillow has a history. You can finish the dreams of those who've slept there. And that is why Sera brought her pillow with her from Italy. The whole town of Frank saw it the day her train pulled up to the station, when faces and luggage began to spill out of the carriage windows. Passenger bags, hat boxes, huge cheeses shaped like hat boxes, sausage crates, cutlery wrapped in hand-embroidered sheets and blankets, even babies were tossed out to waiting arms while the train rolled toward the station house. And where was Pep?

Sera didn't see him. She wouldn't know for years that he was at a crap table winning back their house when she threw that pillow from the window, only to hear it explode under the train's steel wheels. The rest of Frank watched a plump, dark-skinned woman with an oval face, a red and green scarf around her head, emerge from a cloud of pale feathers.

The pillow was an old one, made soft by the many years it had been passed down, starting with Sera's grandfather, a muleteer cheese-maker and pigeon-lover who kept only white birds. During his deliveries two birds travelled with him in a bamboo travelling case. Every day, by mid-afternoon, he decided what kind of pasta he wanted for his dinner—gnocchi, tagliatelle, fusilli, cappelletti, linguine or tortellini—and sent home his decision tied to a bird's leg. His name was Domenico, or just Nico to his friends and customers, who believed that when his birds died they became part of his afternoon meal. The feathers, they knew for sure, went to fill his mattress and pillows.

He told Sera—and anybody else who would listen—that he had won her grandmother's hand in marriage in twenty-nine days by walking past her house, through the main piazza and down to the sea, sprinkling bird food down his pant leg from a hole in his pocket. A man who flies with birds cannot help but be loved, he said, describing the coloured flocks of pigeons and darting sparrows that followed him wherever he went. He tucked both hands in his pockets and bounced a little in his gait, without even a backward glance to the frenzy of birds that swooped from the sky to his heels. When he wanted them to wait for him outside a fruit market he would spread a pile of crumbs and seeds by the entrance with a casual shake of his leg, and make his departure only when the birds were looking restless for more food. One crumb on his shoulder guaranteed at least three birds taking turns to see if there was anything left there worth eating.

Week by week he needed less food to hold their interest, and by the time Sera's grandmother agreed to a stroll in the piazza, the pigeons knew him so well that they would wait for him even without the seeds. They paced on rooftops, window ledges and clotheslines, bobbing their heads with each step and repositioning themselves for a better spot to watch for Nico bursting from his house in the morning wearing a purple vest. The vest was a present from another pecorino cheese maker, the traditional colour worn by only the best sheep herders in southern Italy and, more important for Nico, perfectly visible from the sky.

It was on one of the brightest days in May that Nico, with one hand slung in his pocket, stepped out of the doorway of his father's house and wound his way through narrow cobble-stoned streets toward the centre of town.

Pigeons, sparrows and the occasional seagull kept some distance away when he met with Roma, his future wife, in the Piazza del Popolo. He spoke to her in a quiet, calming voice that made both Roma and the birds feel more at ease with each other. And he slowed his gait a little more than usual to let the finches catch up along the ground beside him. They darted bravely between the pigeons and gulls, so that, collectively, the birds seemed to be walking with Nico, instead of following him. They were a feathered arc of bodyguards.

After the turn of the fourteenth century, he said to Roma, when Europe realized the end of the world would not come as was forecast, the captain of each town in Italy had a square built for his people, a Piazza del Popolo. All of Italy began to come out of their houses, their cloisters. They met with neighbours. They strolled through their square and talked about tomorrow for the first time in their lives. They stopped painting stone-faced portraits, waiting for death in lifeless, cold rooms. They took their first tentative steps out of their frames, toward the Renaissance, life and movement.

In this way Nico told her about the history of the piazza they walked through, a piazza she had visited almost every day of her life but never knew. He was encouraged by finishing one story and seeing her smile, so he dropped some extra seeds from the hole in his pocket to treat his birds and told her another. Most of his stories, histories really, grew into lies that she could spot almost immediately, but they both enjoyed the play of remembering forgotten origins, true origins or false ones.

When they walked past a fruit market Roma herself got into the game, and told him that inside every red Sicilian orange was the blood from the peasants who died under their trees during Garibaldi's conquest of Sicily. Can you see their veins? That is why, she said, without waiting for him to answer, the hill towns still call them Garibaldi oranges.

Maybe, Nico said, they are that colour because Garibaldi's Red Shirts won over even the oranges.

The birds followed them from the piazza to the Municipio, down the stone path to the port and finally to the Wall of Tears where wives waved goodbye to their husbands bound for Napoli, Genoa and America. They talked the whole time they were together and, reaching the sea, able to go no further, they turned around, startling the birds behind them from the ground into the air.

The seeds, evidence of his extortion, were gone, but when Nico's eyes retraced the path from where they'd walked, he saw something far worse. For Nico, that moment was the one where he thought that he nearly lost Roma. For her, it was precisely the moment that drew them together. In front of them, and all the way up the stone road back to the

Municipio, she saw a steady path of bird droppings, like trails of primrose.

At first, Sera didn't care about her grandfather's tricks for love. She was too young when she heard those bird stories and besides, the pillows interested her more than anything else. She would drag one that was bigger than herself to her little brother's room, peel off the pillow cover and climb inside the case for an afternoon nap, on the floor beside his crib.

The pillow necessarily came with her, dragged this time across an ocean, two countries, a mountain chain and *almost* safely past a pair of train tracks to Frank, Alberta. Feathers smattered over the waiting crowd in slow motion and fell on them like tired confetti.

And where was Pep? Again: dealing a hand of something with one-eyed jacks, no doubt. The rest of the town was open-mouthed and watching Sera descend with a scarf and a smile from a white train on a snowy day in August into a town of coughing, wheezing ghosts.

By the time he finished with the cards, she'd picked up all of her grandfather's feathers.

*

Pep, within the confines of Sera's dream, slept soundly while his house crumbled and finally rolled to a standstill. Sera's pillow protected him, even if he was flung from one side of the room to the other.

Hours later, when the world had returned to normal and the sun was rising over the same Frank as he'd gone to sleep in, when the thirty-year-old slide of boulders was, once again, lying at the edge of the town, Sera was still picking out feathers, plucking Pep's backside with a pair of tweezers and wishing she'd married someone who didn't live in a mining town, someone who didn't breathe coal and dig into mountains for a living.

She held a battered tin strainer as she pulled the feathers from her husband's backside. In the afternoon she would wash them, then put them outside, in the sun, to dry.

*

The only holiday that could be named for a miner is Groundhog Day, a day for seeing shadows and burrowing back into the earth for another six weeks. After most mine blasts, the miners who come out of the dark—dead or alive—go back in, one way or another. Most seem to be digging deeper tunnels into more elusive mines. Some, whom Celi knew, drowned in the mine, then were carried out by rescuers who put them back into more proper graves called hallowed ground. The earth is always just as coal-ridden and rocky as the ground they come out of, but the short, white fence that surrounds all of their graves keeps them together, corralled and quiet, for another, later escape. While other men may sleep five feet away and are able to walk out on their own legs, the drowned miner just keeps dreaming. Methane enters his nostrils. He rolls into a shallow puddle and drowns in the dark. On the outside, he is always remembered as the young Valentino, the spitting image, people say, smiling, adding that he took more care of his hair than anyone in the Pass—his girlfriends included—or that he spent more time in the wash-house staring into mirrors than in the mine digging into a coal face. Every time, no matter who he is, the drowned miner is always remembered as one of them dressers. He was a clothes-horse, they say, all dolled up, or all gussied up, a going concern. Jeez you should have seen him. He was a handsome one, that one. A regular Valentino. *When they die they are all saints.* But the ones who live to see the outside of a mine blast literally walk out and never look back. Men like Pep spend the rest of their days doing errands all over the Pass or painting their houses, gardening and such. Another man Celi knows delivers pizza just so he can be in his car and moving. He hardly speaks these days, but seldom does he have to. Nobody asks him twice why he'd come out of the mine to work for a bare minimum; his car answers that question for him. The methane is impossible to smell and, for those men, just as impossible to forget. Every one of them is haunted. And every one of them seems to haunt the Pass, Pep included. Celi knows the gas is swirling around him. (The faint ringing in his head didn't start with Fina's boot.) But the pitch, he thinks, is high enough for the fans to blow clean air to them. With the brattice clear, the gas always has somewhere else to seep. It doesn't bunch up into pockets. They have to stay low and wait, just wait. If they were in a blast, trapped behind rock, he might have started digging, no matter what his chances. That seems strange now, considering there isn't anything but darkness between them and the outside. But he would have taken the risk of sparking the gas and starting a fire. He would have used up his air, if not exploded the coal dust. He would have scraped into rock that had already fallen and turned to fragments. He would have looked for other routes out of the mountain, digging anywhere, even upwards, like the miners who escaped the Frank Slide blast. That was digging. Must have been slower than digging fresh: the air would have gotten to the coal and the lumps would be hard, heavy, but he would have tried it too. Some gold miners in Kalgoorlie, Australia, he'd heard, dug right up into the town pub's basement, drank their shift away and still made it back through their tunnel to hand in their tags. They only got caught when a few too many of them started falling over in the wash-house. So why, Celi thinks, does this seem so much harder? The answer *Because they had lights* comes to him just as loudly as if Fina had said the words himself. The digging is hard in the Pass. The mines are dark and gassy. If you don't have to move, it's smarter to wait. So they keep talking. Celi talks to keep thinking clearly. He talks for a lot of reasons, none that is decided or agreed upon immediately. But just the talking helps each of them, while they wait for Pep and the morning to appear. He can feel it helping, even when they fight over the noises that interrupt the stories, their voices barely audible beside the timbers that groan and drip in the dark. Even if Celi's voice tapers off into a drizzle, they are listening to a real voice, a shade above the other ones. And Fina speaks some too. More and more, thinks Celi, he takes his turn. Without light to guide their voices they speak right through each other, until the words reach the ear they're meant for, and the echo is finally severed from the real. All these voices start to make sense to Celi. He can sort them out, attaching a human face to one, ripples to another and timbers to the rest. His mind stretches the sounds to their respective mouths like chewing gum.

*

Pep didn't get all of his scars working in mines.

In the months that followed he survived hundreds of Frank slides, probably the most remarkable achievement he ever had, and he did it with the help of Sera's big toe, her sturdy ankles and her knack for plucking ruffed grouse, pigeons and farm chickens.

Even that—her big toe—was beautiful in a soft, pudgy sort of way. Her photos proved she wore her weight with dignity. Two of those photos Pep used in place of bookmarks, hidden in the leaves of a book on proper housecleaning and table etiquette:

—Don't shake your napkin out with a flourish;
unfold it and spread it neatly across your knees. Raise
one corner of it to your lips as the occasion demands.

He wouldn't need those books after she left him.

One shot, a late one, showed her to be a sturdy woman with strong ankles and soft ample breasts, bigger than most people remembered. She was heavy in that one but it suited her, really, being a full foot taller than Pep. Her hair was black and pulled back, braided probably, and she wore her face like a shield's calm challenge. She was leaning forward a little, as if nothing could surprise her, or make her raise her eyebrows. Try it and she looked as if she might lean still closer to the camera and say: I can raise my eyebrows higher than you, my friend. Don't even bother.

But, at the same time, there was something soft about her looks, especially around her eyes. Her bushy eyebrows had matching lashes that swept more than they blinked. Her brow stretched across her forehead and furrowed when she was upset. You could have strung those eyebrows up into buns if you'd wanted to, or wrapped them around yourself to keep warm. Her face was that soft, her cheeks that round. And she had a wide, solid chin.

Pep, in the photo, was himself: stiff and already dazed by the flash. It was impossible to tell if he was happy or not, but he looked secure, not smug. He looked protected.

The other photo Pep wedged between two pages in *1001 Useful Household Helps, Hints and Recipes.* Sera was sentenced and imprisoned between the chapters on "The Treatment and Care of Books" and the title page for "The Care and Cleaning of Carpets, Rugs and Mattings":

—Never wet your fingers to turn over a leaf.
—Never allow your books to get hot, as the board may warp, and the leather may crack.
—Never put them on a shelf high up near the ceiling of a room lighted with gas, as the results of gas combustion are highly injurious.
—To remove ink stains from a book apply oxalic acid

on the tip of a camel's hair brush and then soak it up
with blotting paper.

—The fumes of a match will remove berry stains from
a bookpaper or engraving. A few drops of oil of
lavender will save a library from mould. One drop will
save a pint of ink.

—Never turn down the corners of a page. Always use
a regular bookmark. The simplest, and one of the best,
is a card as large as a small visiting card. By cutting this
twice longitudinally from one end almost to the other,
you will have a three-legged bookmark which rides
astraddle on the page, one leg on the page below and
two on the page you wish the book to open at.

The next page, on the other side of Sera, had a sketch of a
magic carpet flying through dust. And then:

—Beat carpets on the wrong side first.

—If ink has been spilled on a carpet, immediately wash
it out with sweet milk, after which sprinkle with white
corn meal. Leave it overnight, and in the morning
sweep it up, and the colours will remain bright.

—Snow can be used as a rug cleaner by taking rugs
outdoors in the snow, on a cold day, when the ground
is crisp and hard: spread carpet out, right side up, and
throw snow all over it. With a broom, sweep the snow
around and around till it finds the deeply seated dust.
Then beat.

Just as the book described, Pep had taken a card—her
photo—and sliced it twice along the bottom edge, so that her
legs could truly straddle the pages.

The picture itself showed a smiling, older Sera, with the
same solid ankles, still buxom, but her hair was loose and
straight, stretching to touch her shoulders. Both of those

photos were black and white, of course, not that it would make much of a difference if they were in colour. Sera looked as though she wore the same long dark skirts, in sensible earth tones, no matter where she went: to church, or to bed.

The unusual thing about that photo was the horse that she stood beside, and the hurried grin on her face, as if the animal were a celebrity she was finally posing with just before he signed his autograph, on her palm, *Fondest memories, Charlie.*

*

But if Sera dreamed about the mountains of the past crumbling the tunnels and towns of the Crowsnest, about walking to the sea followed by birds, about the sea crashing into the Crowsnest and washing her away from the faded photographs she had yet to take, then it could be said that Pep also dreamed. The only reason why he did not dream at night, or in the recesses of his waking imagination, was because his mining was a dream: the rivers of gas that flowed through mountains gave him plenty to think about. The tunnel's floor drifted, heaved and defied gravity while his men erected timbers to hold Pep's rooms in place. And that seemed mysterious enough.

Almost every miner would say the same: there was no use in dreaming anything or anywhere else. If you started dreaming about something other than your job, you got careless. You got killed. Or you hurt someone else. Most miners probably wouldn't admit to the thought that they too were sailing in seas not unlike Sera's, but the gas was more concrete to Pep than imaginary waters. It was more real because it penetrated real rock and bubbled out the real coal and gave him real money. What more was there to think about?

*

And yet Pep did think back to those photographs in their house, and the seeming dust of age that came to settle over them. He thought about how the photos faded even between unopened pages. He thought about a time when they were both happy in this house and the only thing that kept them apart were the bed sheets that Pep, a man who moved through mountains, could never seem to part.

*

If Pep dreamed about anyone before Sera went missing, before Sera existed, it was about his mother. Teresa used to tell Pep that his brothers wouldn't come around the house to see her because of him. No Ma, he'd tell her, you just raised a helluva family, that's all.

And she knew that, he'd say to himself after she died. In the end, she knew:

The night she died she called him in the night at about three o'clock. *Go get some water for me.* Shit. She could get it herself. She could walk around all right. Well after a while I finally did get it. I went in the kitchen and I got it for her and she said sit down, I want to talk to you. I sat on the side of the bed and we talked for a few minutes or so, maybe more. Finally, I said Mom I gotta go to sleep. She said no, wait for a minute I want to talk to you. She said you must forgive me. I knew what she was talking about for her to keep me for so long you know. I was close to thirty or so. Well, I said, Mom, forget it. It don't matter. And she kissed my cheek. Shit! Surprised the hell outta me. I don't remember her ever giving me a kiss before. I mean she must have when I was little but I don't know. Anyway, she died that night and she knew she was going to. In the morning I passed by her bedroom to make a pot of coffee and I didn't hear her breathing. She was a heavy breather, my mother. Well she was old, eh? I didn't take no notice until after a while, then I went in to check on her. I said, Mom, what the hell's wrong this time. And she was dead. Well I cried for half an hour there and then. After that I went down the street to my brother's house and said you better call Tony and tell him the old lady's dead.

The next night wasn't much of a vigil. Nobody came. Pep washed her face twice, put her in her wedding dress. He spread out her hair to the sides—something he'd never seen before—and sat up with the old lady for most of the night. She was dolled up enough for a wake, so was the house; he saw to that too. He bought a couple of candles to put by her bed. He knew enough to keep them lit until they burned themselves out. They did that at wakes, he'd heard. There was a bottle of rye in the kitchen for guests, a few more chairs squeezed around his small table, some Fig Newtons on a plate. But Pep was more surprised that he didn't dip into the bottle himself than by the fact that nobody came to pay respects.

One hell of a family he had, one hell of a family. Then he'd shake his head and sit up in his chair: a hard wooden one with curved legs. Maybe it was because of him, he thought, but that shouldn't have stopped the bastards from coming. It never failed: the whole bunch of 'em were dead on their feet, stupid from the kneecaps up, with more gall than bladders. If there was any more money to be found they'd be around, but the old lady had given it all away. She thought it would make them visit, Pep figured. But he knew better. Penniless, she didn't leave them enough for them to pay their respects.

He sat there all night. He slept a little only near the end, closer to four, maybe five. What did it matter? Nobody came. A year later he sailed for Italy and met Sera.

Pep shook his head and pointed to his empty coffee cup.

*

Something beside Celi splashes. (Then it is suddenly quiet in the tunnel.) *He lives alone?* Yeah, but before Sera came over he took care of his mother. I think the old bugger lived with his mom for thirty years. Can you believe that? *I thought she was alive when he married Sera.* Nope, says Celi. Sera might have thought she was though. She might have had the feeling that the old lady was still around. It's bloody tough moving into somebody else's house. You don't suddenly come into a place and make it yours. Sera had her work cut out for her. Pep wasn't much for cleaning. Took a lot to get used to the place, I imagine, what with Pep living there, taking care of the old lady until she died. But Sera cleaned up the house, just like you said. She made it her own. They all do that when they first come over. They think they can get rid of the dust.

*

Sera didn't think about Sunderd because he was a doctor. She may have fancied herself a kind of physician, in sparing Pep countless deaths by feathers, but Sunderd wasn't the only person she knew who wasn't a miner.

No, she thought about Sunderd because, like him, she'd felt something altogether different that day at the mine, as if she'd seen something else besides a horse being carried out of darkness. Sunderd did too: his knees buckled in response. When Sera saw the horse she felt that something glowing next to her, then inside her, a light she hadn't seen since she'd burned her eyes and watched all those letters, Pep's letters, burning in snow. Sera couldn't understand the feeling. She just remembered closing her eyes, seeing a bright flame in the centre of her vision and loving its warmth. When it stayed inside her she was more than happy; she was vindicated, almost liberated from Pep's past.

When Pep, the horse and that woman's hand came together outside the mine she'd felt the same way. What had

begun in the snow was repeated, continued, beside the mine.
She felt the same hot sting of shocking him awake, when he
least expected it.

*

The moon spotlighted a lamp and cast a distorted shadow
against the wall next to Sunderd's head. Tonight every noise
made him wince; his senses felt brittle and charged. His bed
sheet and two blankets pinned him to the mattress, not that
they were so heavy he couldn't rummage for a hand and lift
them away, but he didn't want to feel the sheets scrape across
his dry skin.

His whole body was dry and weak. Every bit of nail,
tooth and skin on him, right down to his smallest pore, and
even the hair sticking out of those pores, felt hollow and
parched, ready for the glint from his window to set a brush
fire in motion. A moonbeam alone was enough to smoke a
flame into existence. But pulling his blankets away to feel
cooler air meant dragging his arms up too far from his
stomach, so Sunderd stayed still. His hands felt good below
his navel, covering his stomach, calming his insides.

He kept his mouth wide open. He breathed carefully,
deeply. Air from his lungs swirled quietly through gaps
between his teeth, cool air coming in, warm air going out.
One inhalation chilled the outside of his teeth, while the same
breath's exhalation warmed the roof of his mouth. Every five
minutes he pursed his lips and breathed through his nose to
save his teeth from cracking. He didn't have enough saliva
to lick his lips.

Sunderd tried to ignore the scrape of his chest hair
against the sheet. Each breath reverberated through his
nerves like a breeze through autumn leaves. He looked at the
lamp's distorted shadow on the wall and thought he saw a
crane, maybe a pregnant woman, standing on one leg.

Only inside his head was he wet and swimming—swimming badly or drowning well. Bubbles in his brain circulated through the blood near his temples and moored in narrow passages for a second or two. Then the bubbles seemed to squeeze by in a rush—in a sudden, long-awaited, difficult birth—only to get caught again a fraction of an inch later. It wasn't so painful as it was maddening. His thoughts just couldn't get anywhere. His brain felt huge and at the same time jerky. His mind wobbled and lumbered unsteadily toward a light, a smell or an idea like a chubby, cranky toddler. His skull might as well have been surrounded by another shell, a watermelon perhaps, or a spaghetti squash (yellow, bruised and overripe), anything that kept him one room removed from the real world and drifting resolutely in his own.

From within his melon's room, and from the melon within this dark room, Sunderd could hear echoes from another room, more like the push of voices against his walls: people were talking, spitting out words that bounced off their listeners and rebounded toward him. There was the unmistakable cacophony of a laugh, a pause, then another laugh. But maybe they were shouting at one another; suddenly he couldn't tell. He could hear his name, he thought.

But that was all. The rest would wait. I can wait, he thought. I can wait for sleep. I can wait for the bubbles to leave.

In the afternoon, the next day, he was whole again. He could think. His head had shrunk back to its proper size, maybe a little smaller; it felt tight. The bubbles in his brain were gone, or dispersed evenly through his blood. He wondered whether it was all only a headache. Was that the reason? He got migraines so infrequently, once a year at the most, that he never realized what was happening to him until a whole throbbing afternoon had gone by. Until his brain was on the verge of shutting itself off. He just kept wondering to himself: *What the hell is going wrong today? What the hell is going wrong?* He thought (as if he'd just learned a new medical term): They call that bubble-squishing-through-tighter-and-tighter-funnels-in-your-brain, through your *noodles*, a headache.

But it wasn't just a headache. It was much more. And the liquor hadn't helped. That much was obvious. He wouldn't be clinging to the wet sheets of a strange bed—beached and worm-eaten—this late in the day if it had been good for him. He didn't recall consciously making the decision to drink, to reach for a glass—no, the bottle, that's right—to twist the cap off and raise it to his lips. He didn't decide any of that any more than he decided to take on a job better suited for an undertaker or a crow. Scavenging the dead: that's what he felt like. That's what he remembered. The scavenging.

He could feel his Adam's apple jutting out of his neck with every swallow, or before every swallow, when he cleared the bile from his mouth. It built up and caked his lips. The taste of dry paste was still thick in his mouth. The skin on his lips was thick too.

But what he could remember from the day before—was it just yesterday?—wouldn't fill a shot glass. There were bodies, miners who needed to be found before anyone would go back to work, hands that he pulled from the sink, and hands that pulled him from a horse.

The horse.

And there was a woman.

SIX

There are places inside a person where one can hide, harbours where old men sit on wooden fish crates and mend the night's nets with invisible, glinting needles.

In Sera's harbour there was a long, solid dock, made from huge cedar poles. The dock felt more rooted to the earth than the thin stretch of nearby gravel that was the earth. The gravel then faded into a path that led her to town, to voices, to other people, but it was seldom used. Sera was alone. The fishermen, on their crates, did not count as 'others' because they were mending her nets. They were part of her harbour. Their thick fingers—she could not follow them fast enough—moved quickly when they found a tear, but what she liked best were those times when they found a gash too large or too frazzled to sew together, so they used knives to tear away more of her net and start again. Their knives had wooden handles that could float in water. She thought the blades were sharp enough to cut the waves themselves and sliver them into icicles, but the old men never lost their knives to the sea.

Their fingers spidered every inch of her nets, picking away fragments of coral the colour and size of her fingernails, knotted reeds and brown bits of sponge they called the sea's milk, *latte di mare*. The old men found fish bones tangled in the net's eyes, victims of other predators, and sometimes mystery bones that belonged to no animal of sea or land. And they threw them all, bones, reeds, fingernails, all the shards from her nets, everything, over the dock's edge into the water.

They weren't surprised by anything they found. Their smooth faces never changed and they never looked at anything but the net and its collection of knots. The instant something was pulled from the net it was flung, tossed nonchalantly over the edge, while Sera stood wagging her head back and forth, from her nets to the water, squinting at the sinking images for clues to her past.

This was how she read her dreams while she dreamed. *This is how she sees.*

*

I once asked a girl to marry me, says Celi. Didn't know what the fuck I was doing. (Fina is silent, probably nodding.) But now. . . . *Can you hear that?* Forget it. It's nothing. (There is a blank moment where Celi struggles with thumb-like fingers to pick up the thread of his story.) See I forgot to ask her papa. By the time I got over to see him he'd already found out. All he said to me was Christmas is a fine time to be born but it's a helluva time to get married. Guess that ended it for her. For me too, I suppose. After a time I just quit seeing her. Got to be difficult, you know. I'd drive there, though, couldn't stop my truck from going over there, then I'd have to veer off at the last possible turn just to avoid seeing her house, or her house seeing me. Hey, and that turn-off was the church parking lot; I figured God wanted me to go repent or something. Celi laughs at his own joke. Never figured myself a church-going guy before now. (Fina doesn't ask who the girl was.) Celi dated a lot of girls around the Pass: more than most, by his own admission, and there weren't too many to choose from either. Some brides needed a translator to understand the vows they were committing to memory. From Slavtown to Dagotown, it didn't matter: there just weren't enough to go around. Celi feels good telling the story. The gap is filled, the thread—for the moment—busy. Once every so often he knocks the bottom of a shovel against the pile of rocks—warning Fina ahead of time—but they hear no response. He doesn't expect one. The mountain is empty. The noises they send through the tunnel skip down the thirty-degree pitch, scraping cobbles from the cap rock, sliding down man-ways and coal chutes, only to fade from their hearing and sink into silence.

*

A train whistled by.

She was Italian; Sunderd knew that for sure. Her hair wasn't just black, it was thick, with a rope-like coarseness he'd seen trailing behind only Mediterranean immigrants. She'd pulled it back into a lazy cord of dark knots, not much longer than her shoulders. He remembered she looked warm; the afternoon sun cast a low, uncritical light on her face, leaving her skin firm and olive-coloured.

Her clothes were loose, he thought, perhaps brown. His mind's eye saw her trailing a rosary. No, that was the other woman's, the woman who'd struck the miner. He was sure.

The woman who came to the miner's rescue had a calmness about her, something steady in her eyes that balanced her, made her buoyant and level, while Sunderd drowned noisily. The day before yesterday wasn't just a simple drowning. He had tried to grasp the water with wide-spread fingers. He had thrashed, gulped down self-propelled water, and sunk to levels nobody would ever forget.

A horse for chrissakes. How the hell could a horse live that long? He still couldn't believe it. If he didn't see it come out of the mine with his own eyes. . . .

But he had. He'd seen the horse almost two weeks after it should have died. The tapping noise was real too—a thought that struck him just as incredibly as the ghost horses that live in abandoned fire stations. The firemen might be gone, the horses retired, their carriages modernized into fire engines, but the horses could still be heard stirring, clacking their hoofs in their stalls, right before every fire. It seemed that imaginary.

Sunderd was still in bed, thinking about everything that he had gone through and everything that had gone through him in the last two weeks. The bed became comfortable, finally, two days into his stay. He started to feel safe and protected. It was as if the world had stopped turning when he came to the Sanatorium, when he was carried here. That part was the most blurred, as if he'd slowly faded from the mine site and ended up here, in bed.

But the short stay—his *soggiorno obbligato*, as they said in Italian—did him good. His room was on the second floor of the three-storey building, immediately across from the railway tracks. The train whistles didn't bother him at all; instead, they drew him out of himself, as did the sulphur baths he took in the hospital's basement. He'd had only nine of the baths, but they freshened his skin and cleared the solitude from his brain. He felt the sulphur push the water right through him.

Or perhaps it was the company of actually living patients, with all their limbs intact, that did him good. Watching them walk and talk kept his mind busy, away from his missing bottle. He saw himself, briefly, as one of them. A patient. For the first time in his life he might have felt euphoric giving a doctor's responsibility to someone else. He might have enjoyed, suddenly, being out in the world.

In the wash-house, somehow, he had tricked himself through the days, imagining what was going on outside so he could forget whatever his hands were doing. At the Sanatorium, his hands were empty. He didn't have to do anything. The water washed and opened his pores. And here, he let it run through his fingers.

Sunderd put his head back against the tub's edge,

enjoying the cold metal on his neck and the steam rising to his nostrils. Sulphur smelled nothing like the human body, he thought, nothing like fire or burnt blood or human pain. There wasn't a word to describe it, at least none that he knew. Sulphur came from the most foreign place he could imagine, a place that only a horse had glimpsed: the earth. And yet it cleansed.

There were ten tubs in all, each six feet long and three feet wide. Half of them were outside, beside the building, the water having been pumped through the basement's boiler room then out to the tubs. Sunderd himself had pushed many of his patients into the galvanized vessels. It usually took some convincing. He'd sent tuberculosis patients, arthritic octogenarians, back-injured miners, recuperating war veterans from First World War gas attacks, new mothers, even a farmer looking for a warm spot to leave some motherless duck eggs. Every one of them felt better for it. He was surprised he hadn't prescribed it for himself.

But then, healthier folks generally stayed as far away from the Sanatorium as they could. He was guilty of that paranoia too. Washing one's pains away usually meant sending the pain somewhere else: the water as carrier rather than healer. He knew that was why passing trains were practically the only visitors they had.

But that was fine. Sometimes he waved. Sunlight and water flickered across his skin. A breeze stole the steam from the top of his chest. A whistle blew.

Sunderd just sat in the water and listened, for the first time in weeks, to something else besides himself.

＊

Voices from the dark: that was back when I fancied myself an entrepreneur, Celi admits. Mister Five-and-Dimer turned Restaurant Entrepreneur Extraordinaire. I'd heard that Michel was going to be the Chicago of the North, the biggest boom-town in all Canada. Can you believe that? It was a company town all right, but everybody in the Pass was talking about the money to be made. Hey, it started coming in, too, just like they said it would. Coke ovens, the works. Not like Chicago, mind you. Anyway, I got some of my own money together—I saved enough, didn't gamble it away—borrowed some too, and decided to spruce up the Coleman diner to accommodate all those bigwigs. Figured with all of these wheels riding around, making shit-loads for themselves, I might just be able get hold of some myself and use it to get out of the mine after that blast, once and for all. First thing I did was send for some fresh oysters. Atlantic oysters. They liked that food. So what do you think happened? Never mind, I'll tell you. I sent for those oysters, had them packed in ice and the next day they started making the trip—by train. Shit, they hardly made it into Montana. The conductor got a call from his man in the caboose, that he was suffocating or some such thing and passengers were asking questions: Are we on the right train? If we're in the Rocky Mountains why does it smell like the ocean? Where the hell are we? The train stopped and dumped all my oysters. So much for that brilliant idea. But what happened after that was the sorry part. A few people got to hear about these oysters, that they were coming, what was happening to them, you know. I stayed pretty quiet about the whole thing, but that didn't stop some from getting wind of it, like the story itself had a smell to it I couldn't quite keep secret. One guy from Blairmore, his name was Pic, he went out there to actually see what had happened. He saw a black bear had gotten into one of the cases, but this guy, this Pic, scares him off and cleans out the rest of those stinking oysters, brings the shells back to his place in Blairmore. You follow me? Next day after that, this Pic was selling Fresh Oysters, opened up and right in their shells. Soon as they were eaten, the shells went right back to the kitchen. Hell,

Pic went through thousands of cans. None of those yokels knew the difference. Most of his oysters were even smoked, for chrissakes, and that lasted right up until people started taking the shells home as souvenirs. Suppose I was too honest to last long in business. It just took one train and a nice day for me to find that out in a quick hurry. So I went back in the mine, where I stayed. What the hell else is there to say? Some guys are better off in the mine. I'm a miner, what more do you want? *Time to leave, I suppose.* Yeah, said Celi, it's about time for me. It's almost pension time. You think I want to sit around here listening to timbers talk longer than I have to? *You can hear them?* Sure I can hear them; they're creaking is all. Always have, always will. Long as you got the pressure building up you're gonna get the creaking. *But you can hear them talking.* Never mind about the timbers. I've heard a lot of things, seen a lot more and forgot more than you'll ever know. I've seen guys working in these mines for thirty-five years. I've seen them come out of the mine one day—at the end of a shift—and just say thank you very much, and not come back. Just like that. I've seen it happen.

*

When he first met Sera, Pep was on a train that descended Italy as slowly as a spider, down the arch of Calabria. On one side of the train the Mediterranean either lashed at the scribble of coast they traced or left its bays smooth and unbroken. Only towns punctuated their journey. And they stopped at every station.

On the other side, across from Sera, Pep watched fleeting staircases of vineyards, some rows tended or owned by different peasants, others uniform in colour and draped by vines that swept over the earth. They were grizzled brown nets, alive and pulsing with freshly caught grapes, from top to bottom. The nearby land was tilled, especially along the coast beside the hillside towns. Steps were cut into the hills as sharp and manicured as those on a pyramid. Bergamot, giant lemon, olive and fig trees lined those stretches between stops, between those hills that pushed the towns closer to the sea, the same hills that would darken the room and push Pep closer, somehow, toward Sera.

They sat almost opposite one another, glancing away to the carriage windows before their eyes met. She'd averted her eyes from him to more than half a dozen bays and inlets. He'd averted his to farms, broken buildings and abandoned churches. Most of the churches were roofless or missing entire walls that had fallen into the ground. Clouds were their pulpits. The remaining churches were more stubborn— despite the earthquakes—and sank into the earth only when the ground eroded beneath them. Natural spring water came up inside the churches and flowed right out their two-foot-high doorways.

But Pep didn't notice these things; he pretended to, but his seriousness betrayed him. Sera knew he was watching her. She could feel him inching closer. Probably nothing would have happened had she not been with her cousin, a sixteen-year-old boy with a face full of smile and an eager handshake.

Bon giorno, the boy said to Pep, even though they had been sitting in the cabin for half an hour already. Pep returned the greeting. Then, while their hands were still wagging, the boy asked Pep if he had a sister.

He is crazy for girls, Sera said in Italian, before Pep could answer.

Pep gave them his name instead and told them he was from America. Sera's cousin asked if he had a sister in America.

Pep shook his head, lying to stop his questions, while Sera quickly swung her arm across her cousin's ribs.

HELLO MY FRIEND HOW ARE YOU? he said loudly, this

time in English. MY NAME IS VITO.

But she was not so easily embarrassed. She dismissed her cousin by not looking at him, switching her attention completely to Pep. And after that he and Sera could talk freely, without avoiding eye contact.

Usually, Pep told her, he sat beside old Sicilian men clutching large paper bags.

That is wise, Sera said, bringing up a finger to pull down her cheek and open her eye wide. Like the fox, she was telling him.

Especially if you are 'making a turn,' travelling alone, from somewhere else, *fuori*. Those old men don't miss a thing. You are safe sitting beside them, safe from thieves who will slice the bottom of your bag when your eyes are closed.

Pep agreed quickly, probably too quickly, he thought, feeling suddenly like her cousin. His Italian was rusty.

A field of sunflowers floated past the window, brightening their cabin.

Girasoli, he said, remembering the word suddenly, smiling, then watching her eyes light up as if the flowers themselves had turned to meet her face.

That was probably why he'd begun to write to her about flowers as soon as he'd returned to Canada. That much they'd shared, from their first hour.

He'd been honest enough about that moment not to write about flowers to any other girls. Sera might not even know that, he thought, for all it mattered. She'd seen, burned and let the wind scatter his letters from those women, but he'd never asked her if she'd actually read them.

He never would.

And yet most of the Pass knew all about that part of their story, one way or another. Thanks to Sera, they'd seen everything. They'd put it all together just as easily as if they'd received shards of those burnt letters in their open mailboxes, their mail growing with each passing breeze. Sera saw to it that faded stamps burnt grey with bits of dark words and charcoaled name fragments ('Seraf', 'Esthe', 'ina') were found pressing their noses against car windows, straddling falling snowflakes, shovelled into tumbling paragraphs across sidewalks and store fronts and frozen into ice that inched and crackled toward the Crowsnest River's banks, fated to drown in the spring thaw when severed words screaming 'hak', 'ah', 'zzle', 'pu', 'ver', and 'woos' swirled free toward British Columbia.

She imagined some of the words snagged like hooks on the tongues of passing salmon, then returned with their hosts to spawn and die. Some were spiked onto spruce trees or entombed inside growing pinecones. They were caught like criminals at the tops of trees, preserved in maple sap and silenced for twenty years while they dribbled down tree trunks. A nail and a bucket released them.

Other words were mashed into bird feeders, were pecked at, nibbled and dismembered. They got drunk on over-ripe crab apples. They left only wayward Ys in the snow. They took wing and flew with hollow bones. Spanning whole skies, the words were pushed away by gusts of air—wind that held them up like clean, blue lines—as far from the Crowsnest Pass as the wind could possibly stretch.

The burnt letters that never reached the ground or water blended with snow and mine dust. The words were ingrained in the air like a smell, little more than dust flecks that could be read only with the aid of a window and a chance sunbeam. Sneezed wet and bitterly into handkerchiefs, they were carried away in other men's pockets.

And the rest of their words Pep would never read again. Sera couldn't imagine where they went.

*

But that was bad luck, Fina says, *if you ask me anything about it. All those letters flying everywhere. It used to be that you kissed your signature at the end of a letter. Did you know that?* Sure, says Celi, sealed with a kiss. I saw a few of those go up in smoke that day too. *No. You have it backwards. Saint Andrew's sign was an X. When you leave an X you're pledging in his name to carry out the promise in the letter, the promise that your letter is true. That part has nothing to do with kissing. It's the names I'm talking about. People stopped kissing their signatures—that's what they're supposed to kiss— and started in on Saint Andrew's. I don't know why.* Celi doesn't know either, but it doesn't seem terribly important. Everything else is important; they're stuck in a goddamn mountain for chrissakes. But he likes where their conversation is taking them. Fina is thinking of something else besides the birds or the methane. They are imagining other places; sometimes he thinks they are almost out of the mine. *Heard that in church,* Fina says, as quietly as an apology. He brings Celi back with a question: *Did you ever see any of those letters yourself?* Yeah, I saw 'em. But I didn't pay them much attention. It'd drive you crazy if you tried to make sense of them, or put them together. The worst part was finding a bunch stuck to my hunting dogs. They looked like they'd been rolling around in charcoal for most of the afternoon. Probably found the pit where Sera burned the letters and just made a day of it. They looked like those spotted dogs, you know, with the polka dots. (Silence.) Somewhere in the tunnel's darkness Celi sees dogs with real words for spots, scratching fleas of Ms into the air. The letters fly back to different places, are read differently. I'll tell you, Celi says, you're right about that bad luck business. Nothing good could have come outta those letters any which way you looked at them. *Well, Sera put a stop to them.* As soon as she found them.

*

It was only later, maybe a week later, after Sunderd made full sense of what happened with the horse, that he remembered who Sera was.

He'd completely forgotten about their wedding reception. One bash was like any of the others he attended in the Pass. He seemed to swim through a fluid evening, then leap to the next, especially in the summer wedding months. But why he was thinking of her now, he didn't know. It wasn't like him to look at another man's wife.

Looking at another man's wife. Why? And why now?

He'd seen men who came home from logging camps, ring the front door bell to their own houses and then run around to the back yard to catch whoever was running out. Yes, it was more of a joke than anything else, but the thought was there: anything was possible. Anything can happen.

The thought itself made him sick, and he was tired of sickness, tired of death. Why he became a doctor was just another 'why' in the course of his life he had yet to figure out. He'd let that happen too, he thought. Medical school just happened. A small-town doctor's life just happened. The mine accidents that he picked up after just happened. We let our lives happen as if we're just growing toe-nails instead of memories. And until now, his only saviour from everything he'd let happen had been the sulphur springs.

Right then, at that moment, Sunderd remembered something, something he'd read about years before and—just like his first meeting with Sera—thought nothing more about, until now. He'd read an article in *National Geographic* about how men found water in the Sahara desert. They found it by tricking baboons.

The baboons were easy to find. They usually loitered around rocky outcroppings and dried-up trees that bloomed for three rainy weeks per year. Even easier was capturing the baboons' attention, which wasn't difficult, given their inquisitive nature. The water hunters—dressed only in a piece of leather that covered their genitals—cut a small hole into a sandstone wall or a tree so that it angled downward into a reservoir a little larger than the hole itself, like the inside of a gourd. Once they dug the hole they poured some ordinary rocks into it with animated movements, trying to make a show of it, without looking directly at the baboons.

Sunderd remembered that the water hunters chanted something, some kind of spell, but here he was remembering incorrectly. All they really wanted to do was build up the baboons' curiosity.

After staring at the hole for an hour or two, the most inquisitive baboon would inevitably put his hairy, coal-black hand into the hole. And once he grabbed the stones, his bulging fist would be trapped. This gave the water hunters ample time to walk up to their self-restrained prisoner and calmly slip a rope around his neck. Shaking the baboon's arm freed him from the trap. Two days and a bag of salt later, the baboon, as fast as he possibly could, led the water hunters to his nearest source of water.

To no one but himself, Sunderd whispered, you have let this trick happen to yourself for too fucking long.

He gave up any medicine that hurt: medicine that involved cutting into somebody or piecing them together for coffins. By giving up the job—the life—he'd hated for so many years, he thought he could throw away the precious bottles he'd protected. His secret, hidden bottles. The Sanatorium helped him with that. He'd rinsed himself clean.

Sunderd gave up the town and moved himself to a shack in the woods closer to Bluff Mountain. By leaving the town he thought he could manage his life more simply. There were fewer things to control, fewer fragments of his life that could ultimately control him. He left everything that he'd fought so stupidly, so stubbornly to hang onto with both bulging fists, all while a noose was working itself around his skinny, stupid neck.

He left it all.

SEVEN

Celi sits up, tries to spread his arms and point to the imaginary masses standing, in the dark, around the tunnel. That place used to fill up, jam packed, I'm telling you. There was a strange colour to that water. It was milky-like almost, and stronger than any springs you find in other places. Mostly you'd see the Finns there; they liked the sulphur baths, well, baths and steam rooms in general. Used to be that every Finn had his own little steam bath, like an outhouse, sitting pretty just behind his house. Some of them could squeeze two, three people in there for one sitting. I went in them. They had these birch branches, with the leaves all taken off, well it was winter anyway see, and they used to take those branches in one hand, throw some water on the rocks with the other hand, then whip themselves with the branch. It encouraged the stimulation I guess. Every Finn in the Pass had one of them steam baths, believe you me. (A loud creak, like a rope's knot being tightened, gives Celi pause to suck in an extra breath.) Anyway, that guy Sunderd wasn't much of a Finn, if he was one at all—Christ he could have been a mixture of a lot of things. There's a lot of different people in the Pass. But he only started going to the San for those steam baths, and hanging around the Finns, after he stuck his head in that pail of oats. Maybe he heard some kind of secret rolling around in the bottom of that bucket. He sure acted like it. The man changed. He went funny, you know what I mean? After that he gave up his practice almost totally. Became some kind of a plant doctor, a naturopath you call them. Only used herbs and special ingredients. There were a lot of those guys, let me tell you. Sunderd might have been the most well known because he was the crazy one who lived alone in a hollowed-out hill, practically just a mound of dirt with no water, no electricity, no nothing. I guess he planned it that way, bought a low house in a hole that was covered with dirt, well, up against a grassy bluff that kind of spread out over his roof. Used to belong to a moonshine-maker, I think. Least that's what they said. Who else would have made a shack like that? Roosterheads—or what do you call them . . . shooting stars—and dandelions grew on his roof in the summer. Winter-time the snow just buried the place, kept him warm enough. Cold days he brought in a horse to keep him warm. Instant heating. In a place like that Sunderd didn't have any competition, that's for sure, being sort of quirky you know, and with a knowledge of medicine to boot, the Pass was pretty well taken care of in terms of witch doctors. That is, if you wanted to eat lemon shavings in dandelion soup for head colds. They all did that for a time. Chicken soup got to be popular in the winters only because you couldn't find the weeds. There were lots of those kinds of remedies. Sunderd used to stop the hiccups by freezing a man's ear lobe with an ice cube. I never believed in that shit. Sawbone doctors of any kind. You know, in Italy, they called them the Mafia of the White Smock. Organized crime is what it is, and they didn't go too bloody far wrong with that name. *Hey. Did you hear that?*

*

Sera, by this time, was walking nights and days. Her trips into the woods, carrying a waxed-paper bundle of salted pork, kept her mind active, filled and swarming with thoughts that carried her, too, on tiny wings away from the Pass.

Pep worked days, now, on the railroad tracks beside the tipple, sometimes inside the mine's entrance, as a gandy-dancer. He swung his hips, shoulders, arms, then hammer, leaning first back then forward, dancing the wooden staff and iron into the ground with a crude box-step. It was a tired, three-day dance contest between cousins instead of lovers. Had the hammer been taken from his hands Pep might have looked like a blind man endlessly and stubbornly putting the same foot forward into the same curb, again and again. Cut his legs out of the picture and he was sitting in a rocking chair. He had a potter's rhythm, or a weaver's: the spikes drove through iron holes into timber logs that stitched up the earth.

He spit marbled, scarlet threads of blood and dust. Lately he'd been coughing up more blood than dust, so the odd move outside the mine felt good to him, despite the drop in pay. In the tunnels he made some big money, even when the mine boss teamed him with four slack-asses to lower his quota.

But suddenly he couldn't give a shit. The blood did that to him. He knew where it came from. He knew why.

All he needed was some outside time, a chance to clean the dust and slivers of coal from his lungs. Fuck it. And fuck the coal company too. He'd be okay. There was still money to be made.

But he didn't tell Sera about the blood, or, for that matter, the gandy-dancing. He kept swinging and stitching, swinging and stitching. The fire in his throat burned until he spat it out, watched it sink into the dirt.

*

Estruscans made funeral urns to look like houses. The Kowloonese buried caskets for only seven years, exhumed them for cremation, then refilled the costly graves with different relatives. Russians drank with their dead, carrying half a glass of vodka to throw into the pit. Himalayans left theirs on mountain ledges, to be carried away by vultures and buried in the sky.

And Roman Christians hid their dead in the ground. Burials were forbidden in the city, so they went to the countryside and dug graves in old lava that hardened—like coal—in contact with fresh air. To be buried near the popes, saints or priests they built multiple levels, digging deeper and deeper, the graves fanning out into a labyrinth of names, a catacomb of privilege.

Nobody, however, is buried in Sera or Pep's grave. Yes, he dug the hole for her missing body, but he also left a headstone for himself. He bought a matching pair of marble rectangular stones and left the date, his date of expiration, blank.

*

Celi has plenty to say about that: Nuts. That's what it is. Why do you want to go putting your own name on a stone when you're perfectly healthy? Pep was worried then, mind you. He probably thought he'd like to die. But I can't figure it myself. At least he didn't build some kind of memorial with a fancy cross. He didn't change that bloody much. Do you think those fancy crosses get them any closer to God? Hell no. Me, I don't think so either. But they must feel guilty or something. I can't blame them; that's just what they believe. Pep's mother was like that. She wasn't educated, see, and it was deep in her culture. She made him promise her that she'd have a big cross and no weeds would grow over her grave. All right. There it is. Concrete all over it and an iron fence around the whole damn thing. He painted it rust-free, you know. Nothing will grow on it and nobody can walk over it. Pep cleaned the gravel and sand and made it himself. Not a crack in it. He's a good worker, that guy, when you give him

a job to do. And he did Sera's and his own goddamned grave
the same bloody way. Only the concrete over his grave is just
bordered, you know, waiting for the words.

*

Whenever he whisked himself past the whore-house, on his
way to town, Sunderd took pictures—mental pictures—of
everything but the women's unmentionables. He saw a plain
red-brick building, two nondescript windows, a back yard
with a large telephone pole, two clotheslines, four huge steel
pulleys and countless pieces of women's underclothing.
Starched bed sheets, pillow-cases, blue, black, white and red
stockings, whalebone corsets, girdles, garters, handkerchiefs,
skirts and dresses flapped in the wind, snapping colours at
Sunderd as he casually swung his head to look.

Sometimes he saw one or two girls in the windows. He
saw them smile. Once or twice he smiled back, but always
he blushed his way past their door, their house, imagining a
red streak in the air behind him.

Their makeup-blackened eyes made their gaze framed
and distant, staring lazily into cigarette clouds like the
window sills themselves. But when they saw him, their faces
opened up. They seemed genuinely happy, not just smiling
to say hello to someone familiar, but happy.

All Sunderd could imagine was their feet, a bare foot or
just a toe, painted and poised beside some pocket change.
That was the closest he could come to matching their pretty
smiles with their profession. Any other part of their bodies
and the two pictures couldn't meet.

But with those mental pictures Sunderd thought he
could prove something very noble about humanity, something that was clearer when he saw it in fragments or shavings
than in the whole jiggling truth. He didn't know what he
wanted to prove, but whatever it was, he thought the pictures

themselves would be enough: smoke pillows, mouthfuls of money, sheets that dripped dimes when they dried in the sun, a naked foot, an empty blue stocking and a smile.

Almost all of the miners went to the peelers. Sunderd had treated day-old injuries on men who used their time off to head right for the whore-house, and then wobble onward, on their sprained ankles, toward his underground shack in the woods. Both places were on the outskirts of town, with just under a mile of gravel and mountain shadows between them. Bluff Mountain, with its rocky ledges cutting into broken tree-lines, looked as badly shaven and scarred as Sunderd's morning patients. Turtle Mountain eclipsed the sun far less, but hobbling beside the rock-strewn mountain slide was like inching through the cross-section of a pale volcano. The top of the mountain was sectioned like a half moon, an orange segment or a Roman amphitheatre. The boulders blanketed down the mountain's face over two sets of forgotten railway tracks. And on the other side, just where the slide met with the Crowsnest River leading to Bellevue and Hillcrest, Sunderd's tree-line began, twenty feet from the mountain's smallest pebbles.

By the time they reached Sunderd the miners were usually so sponged with rye and whisky that they didn't need pain-killers, not that he had any to offer. Instead, he gave them his own hangover mixture of iron sulphate, peppermint water and spirit of nutmeg, which seemed to anchor their brains from drifting too far from their skulls. Besides mixing herbal teas for colds and bowel obstructions, his new life as a naturopath included setting bones and delivering the odd problem baby. Some days the two were not so dissimilar: he could shift a fragmented tibia back into position with the same grace he turned around an unborn, upside-down baby. His fingers could gently prod and knead swellings of all types, urging Nature to take a more natural, smoother course. And so long as his patients' skin remained unbroken, Sunderd felt safe.

He didn't miss the town, the mine or the mine's sinks, so he spent little time away from his house. Some of his patients brought a chicken to pay for his magic fingers, others gave him a basement-hung salami or *salsiccia* sausage, and somehow he kept alive until his garden came up, sprouting more vegetables than he could possibly bottle for the coming winter. When the porcupines ate the last of his bicycle's spare tires he stopped going to town altogether, not that he saw it as a sign, but more of a quiet suggestion that there wasn't a whole lot for him to do there. The porcupines chewed on the leather seat, handlebars, pedals and even the paint, for most of the summer, until any trace of salt, leather or rubber was gone. By fall his bicycle was a rusted skeleton, sinking happily into last year's pine needles.

He wasn't considered a hermit by the rest of the world. Nobody thought he was far enough from town or sufficiently alone to dress him in that name. The only one in the Pass who managed to turn into a recluse was Candles Kramer, who held onto his property beside the Hillcrest tipple while everyone else sold theirs to the mine's owners. The mine wanted the nearby land to store huge volumes of coal until the prices rose. A mining town that depended entirely on keeping the coal dropping from its screens and melting in its coke ovens sometimes lacked a friend to brave popular opinion. And so, within two months, Kramer was completely isolated inside a black whirl of coal chips that was three times the size of his house. From his window he could see perpetual night, glinting and shimmering, when the coal chips reflected the sun's rays, like the stars in a real night's sky. He may have felt like the first astronomer, proving the stars' existence with a pin and a black sheet. His house seemed thrust up into the night like a fist and at the same time sunk deep inside a glittering tomb, with no wind or sound or smell except the dry, hollow odour from stagnant, sitting coal.

Sunderd didn't know how a smell could be propelled without the slightest hint of moisture. The dryness that filled a miner's lungs seemed ready to ignite internally. It was a kind of invisible warmth that reminded Sunderd of walking along a gravel road. Burning coal did the same thing; it warmed a man from the inside out, which left, just as such a heat promised, the black ashes in his lungs. But when coal was stored, cold and amphibian, its smell wasn't so savoury for the lungs, Sunderd's or anyone else's. If anything, it did the opposite of warming the body, and stole the heat. Candles Kramer himself admitted that sitting coal could make your nose run like a son-of-a-bitch. Just looking at coal did that.

And the miners did look. Some of the men would yell down from the banks of the hole at Kramer, working in his garden, and ask him how his lettuce was coming. The lettuce, in fact, did better than ever, without any wind to damage the leaves and only coal to reflect whatever light fell onto the hole's sides. Kramer's pride, as much as the lettuce itself, kept him living in his coal stars for just a month longer, until both his water and his strength to carry it ran out. Sunderd eventually treated him for dehydration, received ten boxes of gigantic vegetables for his troubles and watched Kramer leave the Crowsnest Pass, its coal chips and his cratered house, forever.

He'd been a miner too. Just packed up his car, and left, Sunderd imagined, for other craters.

*

Darkness, creaking and fetid air. Further into their tunnel, timbers reinforce walls that are temporarily braced with planks, sometimes railway irons, though one kind of rot smells like any other. The whole shaft reeks of decaying wood, broken lagging, rusting iron and damp rock. Even the air seems to be decomposing and molecular, like bubbles spreading thin under ice. Celi has checked along the ribbing for firedamp—primarily the methane that trickles out of a rock's pores when vegetable matter decomposes into coal. He knows the gas runs wild across the ceiling. There are moments when he can almost see the methane threading through the darkness above him. When miners stand too high on loose mounds of coal, the effect is simple and immediate. It makes them dizzy and sends them toward the ground with a seeming bounce. The loose coal that they use for stools is soft, when fresh, especially in the newer sections. It is a mattress that catches them before they hit the floor, before they feel the floor.

*

Sunderd, of course, saw Sera walking near his tree-line. Her hunting jacket was difficult to miss. Her lips moved with almost every step, as if her toes were connected to the same puppet string that worked her mouth. But to say she walked anything like a marionette was a mistake. Her feet moved forcefully, decisively. She seemed to know where she was heading, he thought, until all at once she would stop, on the side of a path, and just close her eyes for five minutes at a time. Sometimes she bent down to the ground, as if she was going to trace a canyon in the dirt around an ant or examine her foot's signature in the earth, and then all at once she stood straight up and threw a rock as far as she could. Other times she tossed it over her shoulder, behind her or off to the side in a sudden flurry that shocked him more because of the hatred in her face than the distance of her throw.

On her way by, if she happened to see him, she would nod, but continue onward, following Turtle Mountain's shadow closer than the road that cut through it. She wasn't embarrassed about anything he caught her doing.

When they grew to know each other better, at least by sight, the nods changed to a mutual blink or, from a distance, a casual wave, which was later abbreviated to something still more casual: a finger pointed up in the air like a touchstone for wind. After that, if he came upon her suddenly, squatting in the grass and ankle deep in the shallow end of a pond, they traded hellos or nice evenings. And that would be all, a whole month's conversation.

*

Everyone knows that the Bagnarote sell the wind. For the price of a bag of salt, five thousand lire, they will tie three knots in a string and give it to a sailor. Undoing the first knot grants him a steady breeze, the second a gale and the third a tempest. The Bagnarote will tell you that biting a peach tree will cure a fever only if the branch withers and dies, that sitting on an upturned bucket brings no fish, that seeing three butterflies together brings sickness, that a bothersome moth circling you means a letter is coming. The size of the moth indicates the size of the letter.

Some of the Bagnarote—the luckiest—have moles with long, black, curly hairs on their cheeks. The unluckiest, the witches, have moles above their lips: a bad sign because the marks are above their breath, forever above the wind. All of the Bagnarote bear children without a groan, by themselves and sometimes miles from their homes. After a small rest they will continue on their way, selling the last of their salt and fish before they bring their new babies home. For them, a person who is called 'four-eyes' is not wearing glasses, but pregnant.

Most Calabresi agree that the Bagnarote prefer the labour of childbirth to that of a bath.

EIGHT

Some men take spoons or small pocket knives and, during the course of a twenty-minute story, slowly peel an orange out of its skin—like the story itself—from a single long and twisted rind. In Celi's hands, stories are broken, less pared than they are picked at, sometimes gouged, but always interrupted by timber creaks and moans. As he talks his eyes open and close without a click, without seeing light. Water drips all around him. A noise to his left makes him turn his neck, though he knows he won't see anything. Yes, he says finally, she came from Scilla, Calabria. But she sure as hell didn't fall in love with the sea like you might have thought. Sera's people were farmers for the most part, you know: grapes, cheese and shit. Her grandfather, I told you, drove a wagon, delivering cheese. He was one of those muleteers. Jesus Christ, were you asleep or something? Sera would have spent most of her time around her house. She had work to do and she went to school too, you know, at least for a while. I remember she said once that she looked after her grandmother, Roma, quite a bit, even as a kid. The woman was a little crazy, hard-headed like most Italian grandmothers, I suppose, *testa dura*. She'd go outside and count every grape and hot pepper in the fields just to make sure the farmers weren't stealing from her. Jesus, with the Mafia buying from her and everything. Wasn't too bloody smart to question those kind of customers. Sera's mother had to pay the workers extra just to put up with Roma. In the end, when she

died, at ninety-eight I think it was, she had given away all of
her property, as if she knew she was leaving for some place
and wanted to get there as fast as she damn well could. She
knew a lot of things just before they happened. Right before
Roma died she said, open the door, Sera's coming. And Sera
was on her way up the hill, just ready to come into the house
from school. She hadn't knocked or tried the door; the old
woman just knew. Most of those old ladies could do that, or
thought they could. If you let them they'd pull it over you like
a tent. Hell, for that kind of trick you don't need to read olive
oil in water. You don't have to be one of those women from
Bagnara. A Bagnarota. (Cap rock falls and shatters, slides
down a distant chute and clacks against a wall's wooden
lagging. The sound breaks Celi's story, until Fina picks it up,
continues his thoughts.)

*

Sera trailed after the old woman who waddled through the
house on ankles thick as stove irons. Her slippers clacked and
thwacked rhythmically against the tiled floor, one clack for
three of Sera's little steps. The only other sound came from
the sea, or from the row-boats that strained their way through
the tunnel beneath Sera's house. She heard the boats being
dragged from the water every morning, saw the boats in the
narrow street, leaning against the *casa del vicino*, from her
window. It was cool, and so early in the morning that even
the flies were sluggish, dazed from Roma's sudden burst into
the kitchen and her casual swat to none of them in particular.

Sera needed her grandmother's touch to begin every
day, and each morning she followed Roma, pointing to a
place where a new ailment needed her help: an elbow, the
middle of her back, sometimes her ear lobe. Today it was the
side of her left heel.

Roma let her wait until the coffee was threatening to

bubble out of the stainless steel espresso pot, until last night's bread was warmed and moistened with marmalade, until the table was fully set for the morning's breakfast, with huge cappuccino cups mooning above the bread plates, small knives for carving fruit off to the sides, and a heavy ceramic bowl full of red oranges in the very centre of the table. Then Roma sat in one of the chairs and waited for Sera to drag another up in front of her.

They both relaxed into the morning's ritual: as soon as Sera pointed to her heel, said *qui*, the old woman responded *sì, certo*, as if she'd seen the invisible problem from the beginning. She carefully circled the area with her palms and, with a priest's sober eyes, covered the spot with both her thumbs. A moment later and Sera left smiling and ready for another day.

After that, the kitchen was a noisy, bustling place. Sera's mother took the white, heavier bread from her husband's plate and replaced it with shards from a hard brown loaf, so crispy he needed to dip it in his cappuccino to keep it from cutting his gums. Sera swatted away flies while her grandmother wobbled from the table to the sink with dishes of sliced pears, pecorino cheese and extra milk for Sera's drop of coffee. Others arrived, Sera's sisters, Maria and Anna and her brother, Angelo, all bustling in and out of the kitchen, the morning and her life. But it was Sera's grandmother who stole the morning away from everyone—as she did in most of Sera's dreams—with stories, *racconti* about Calabria.

There was a stillness Sera looked forward to, when the kitchen was finally empty of everyone but Roma, the room itself waiting for her words. Roma brought all her characters into the kitchen, propped them up in chairs or made them small, the size of her finger, and rolled them across the table like the Christmas coins Sera found under her pillow. She talked and nattered in dialect without expecting a smile or answer in return. *You don't have to tell the farmer that pecorino cheese goes with pears.* Whatever she said, her accent sounded more Greek than Italian.

Yet most people simply ignored her. They found not answering less strenuous than sorting out Roma's singsong muttering. If Sera's mother gave Roma any sort of advice, she would only do things in her own way, as she had been doing for years and years, so what did it matter? They left Roma to herself and unfailing, at the end of each day, Roma would say: Poor people, everyone's going deaf.

Sera, however, was happy to spend her day with Roma, if only to paddle after her and steady the swirling of words through the house while her family was at school or work. Roma seemed to touch everything in the course of a day, like a gentle earthquake that shook the dust off every bottle and bowl in the house, yet settled those same objects into more secure and stable places.

As soon as Roma left the room, the whole house seemed to relax and sag a little from its door frames and hinges. Sera could squint her eyes and make the walls themselves bloat in and out, breathe deeply to catch their breath, or stand straight up when her grandmother entered, jolting even the people in their picture frames stiff and awake.

She brought wind into the house.

＊

The Bagnarote believe that if a person dies in the fields by a violent or accidental death, then his spirit will appear, standing in the same place, wearing white robes. The only way of laying the ghost to rest is to send out young boys to approach silently and cover the spot with a barrage of stones.

C'era una volta, there was a time when a visiting Sicilian priest, in his white garments, went to a hill above Reggio to watch the sea. It was Father Angelucci's last day on the mainland. He'd spent eight full days waiting for the wind to die and let the currents alone push the waves into chains of black mountains. If the wind hushed between Sicily and Calabria, the distant hills off Messina could darken the water and make the sea into glass. With the sun on the Calabrian side, and the tide at its height pressing the dark water up in the centre of the channel, the waves could grow into what was called the *fata Morgana*: a fabled watery picture of Reggio where every object existing or moving in the town was repeated a hundred times along the surface of each wave.

But Father Angelucci's time was running to an end. That evening he was to give Mass at vespers. He couldn't wait another day, or for that matter another hour. Though he'd already dressed for Mass, he still had to walk down the hill into Reggio, cross from one end of town to the other, buy a ticket and catch the last day's ferry back to Messina. The two-mile stretch of water between Calabria and Sicily kept their worlds so distinctly separate they spoke different dialects.

He didn't have much more time to wait. In an instant the *fata Morgana* could appear and disappear, so the priest was completely absorbed in the last minutes of his watch. He hardly breathed. He didn't see the young boys creeping up on him from the edge of the hills. He didn't see the stones in their hands. He was simply an outsider who had heard a Calabrian myth and was watching the Strait, waiting for the wind to hush, for the *fata Morgana* to appear for his own eyes. When it came, he'd heard, the vision hovered above the water, spread out on thirty-foot waves that seemed as close to a man's face as his outstretched hand. The enchanted seascape was named for Morgan le Fay, King Arthur's unruly sister, when the waves once rose to tempt the Normans. They'd refused, pledging to cross and conquer Sicily without the aid of magic or waking dreams. But Morgan's name endured far longer than they could have imagined.

Just as Father Angelucci was about to give up his watch, the sun crossed to the forty-five-degree angle it needed to glaze the sea. The wind died. The town, every building, window, tree, hill and the priest himself, was multiplied into thousands of rolling images, each one carried along its own wave, framed by dark crests, an amphitheatre of reflection. The priest was euphoric. He jumped to his feet and watched the first waves tear his white cloak into three even sections.

At the water's edge the sea was black. Only from the hills could his death be witnessed. The stones that hit him glimmered their way across the mirrored channel. Each wave reflected a single stone and swelled beside the others. Father Angelucci's surprised face, his hands above his head, every part of his body shattered across the waves, moving through an equally sundered city. As the mirrored priest rode wave after wave through Reggio, cleaving a slow path through the town, he crossed the channel all the way to Messina. And when his waves broke on the shore the sun's angle changed, with the *fata Morgana* disappearing well before vespers.

Some people said Father Angelucci watched his own death before it happened. Others said that he didn't die, or make his way back to Sicily, because he was seen in his white robes—waiting at the same spot—a few days later.

*

She inherited Roma's ankles, those stove irons, as if they were wrapped in tablecloths and hidden away for safe keeping. Sera found them by accident, roughly ten years into her marriage, when she looked down one morning at her bare feet, and suddenly knew, for the first time in her life, that she was becoming old.

She knew this to be true, with the same quiet self-consciousness she felt when the day pulled her from the night's current. It was that same kind of thought: the one that ran aground at the edge of a dream, every morning, and settled firmly, finally, in her mind:

Oh, this is who I am.

Neither good nor bad, the idea made her do little more than blink. Most times she rolled over.

But she left the next week, for good. Pep, for his part, knew this to be true. He worked it out in his mind a thousand times: she left his house. She left him. His shovel slid, scraped cleanly into white rubble, as if the rocks were frozen peat moss, or snow. She left. The shovel swung and fanned high above the ground, through the air. She left. Then it slipped neatly away from the rocks like a letter from an envelope, spreading the rocks out across the ground, pushing them into another pile one foot high, but long, very long. The new pile turned into a straight bed of whiteness that would, eventually, support evenly spaced rungs of timber, a sprinkle of lime, two iron rails and a train.

She up and left.

*

Sunderd didn't count on the first cold snap. The wind blew colder and earlier that year, promising more gales with a harsher bite. Obediently, September's calendar page turned without a sound, without complaint, and faster than most months. The space between September and October always did seem especially thin to him, transparent, as if just glimpsing the first two weeks of October through the paper could bring him there. Somehow his days were doubled, tripled. The hours overlapped to make four days drift into one. He accomplished almost nothing in an entire morning, counting himself lucky if he completed breakfast by supper-time.

The days were becoming as grey as the horse that he bought to keep himself warm in the winter. Its belly sagging lower than his kitchen table, the horse shifted from one side of the room to the other like a roving couch Sunderd couldn't

quite decide where to place. He did know enough to regulate
the horse's drinking and eating, so that he cleaned the floor
as little as possible, maybe once a week. Wood chips spread
over the dirt floor gave the room a pine scent, kept the horse's
smell from lingering and made picking up the odd miscalcu-
lation much easier. But the horse wasn't inside as often as his
patients thought it was.

Sunderd just hated the cold. And he used everything in
his power to fend it off. His shack in the ground was insulated
fairly well, but he stockpiled great quantities of coal and
wood, candles, newspapers, lamp oil and blankets. He used
the horse only when he felt his fingers were fumbling too
much with the matches, or when he was tired of smoke and
dust. For Sunderd, the horse's warmth was the nearest he'd
ever found to match the heat of burning coal, without burning
anything at all. An overwhelming warmth enveloped him,
pulled him close and did more than cloak his skin with heat;
it penetrated his body as much as a midnight sulphur bath.
The warmth wrapped around his lungs like buttonholes or a
woman's legs. It drew the chill from his body in one last and
final shiver. It was also the closest thing to having someone
around, yet being alone at the same time.

Despite his efforts, spiders were beginning to die, one at
a time, all over his house. One morning he counted ten
spiders, most of them lying on their backs in his kitchen,
surrendering to the coming winter. Two were almost the size
of bottle caps with legs. But the spiders were bottle caps with
their legs bent inward. Upside-down, their legs gnarled right
back to their bodies, like grizzled hands or claws that pierced,
it seemed, their hearts.

To Sunderd, they were suicides for the vestiges of fall.

*

The first time Sera and he went walking together Sunderd

made a mess of it almost immediately. They were barely together for a complete sentence before Sera went to sit on a fallen tree and Sunderd, turning around quickly and seeing her there, blurted out:

For chrissakes don't sit there. The ticks might be out.

He softened his voice, then added: They crawl right through your pants when they're small and suck on your blood.

Sera jumped up right away, but the damage was done. In a single second he felt the whole world swing shut on him like the passing of midnight, New Year's Eve.

Sera, for her part, couldn't have cared less. As soon as she brushed the wood dust and lichen from her skirt she had forgotten the matter completely. It was Sunderd who was bruised and filled with regret. He was the one who was rushing another man's wife. He was the one who had invited himself along for a walk through the woods. And he was the one who felt guilty just thinking about protecting her. That was for her husband to do.

The next moment he was off, remembering—he said— that he'd forgotten to water his horse.

It wasn't until later, two weeks later, that he got up his nerve to talk to her again. He told himself he was waiting until the ticks were gone and the days were firmly planted in October, but the truth was he didn't know when the ticks were out or when they weren't. Magpies were scaring away the sparrows from nearby crab-apple trees, eating the naturally fermented fruit and practically falling down drunk when they landed. The apples splattered tiny red explosions on the ground, a colour that matched the violet-brown hues of fall and the red leaves that fluttered into a quiet brown by the time they reached Sunderd's feet.

Sera's walks, at that time, were more leisurely than before the mine blast. She must have been calmer then. With the cold air settling the ghosts from her past, she may have thought less about Italy and the sea, and felt more resigned to finding herself in the Crowsnest. She no longer woke surprised that she was still in Canada and that Pep was indeed lying beside her.

And yet, *why do you stay here?* was the first question she asked Sunderd, the first question she had ever asked him. She meant to ask him about staying in the woods, not necessarily about his remaining in the Crowsnest, as he thought she'd asked.

He was about to say something about his horse, that he had to take care of it, but that answer seemed foolish to him, especially because he had used his horse for an excuse during the last walk.

I live here, he said.

Sera nodded solemnly, and Sunderd knew she had let him out of an invisible box with that nod. She'd helped him somehow: he felt he didn't need to explain his answer. She was like Mendleman, the town watchmaker, who met him on the street with a question he could never answer. Every time Mendleman saw Sunderd he asked him what the good word of the day was, and then, before an unbearable pause became too much for Sunderd, the watchmaker asked him something different, something meaningless about the weather like: Do you think the rain will hurt the rhubarb? And all Sunderd would have to say is yes, or no. That was all. While Sunderd tried to come up with a word, Mendleman filled the silence for him, sometimes with only a smile.

Sunderd was able to walk in silence for a while, and it felt good to both of them. Sera thought about her grandfather Nico, taking walks with his birds trailing after him. If she had some crab-apples she could do the same trick with magpies, she thought. But she wasn't like her grandfather and she wasn't wooing somebody with bread crumbs. She didn't think of Sunderd as anybody but a bushman doctor, a little lonely perhaps, like her. But that was all. They weren't connected to each other by anything more than a thread of common interest: the mountains, walking in the woods and a horse that didn't die in the mine. Railwaymen in passing trains spoke to each other more than Sera and Sunderd did.

After a while he wanted to say something to her, something that she had never heard before to match the something that he had never before felt. But the words were caught, stuck deep, too deep for him to clasp, in too dark a place for him even to see.

So Sunderd walked. He walked further than he had ever walked without mumbling to himself. He followed Sera's plaid-red jacket down one side of a gully and up the other side, against a twisted line of barbed-wire fence and along a ridge that ended suddenly at two gnarled trees corkscrewed together in dance, before he finally thought of something to say. It welled up in him gradually, until he could see what he was going to say, suddenly, in one incredibly lucid moment.

She was walking quickly on those strong legs of hers, breathing normally. Every so often he glanced down to watch the steady rhythm of her calves, climbing, pushing away the dirt under her feet. No matter how difficult the footing, her head never wavered. She had a grace that he couldn't quite place. And at one point he seemed hardly able to keep up with her without panting wildly, so when he finally spoke, it was his horse, again, that gave Sunderd his excuse to stop and say:

If you were a horse I'd buy you.

That was the closest Sunderd ever came to telling Sera that he loved her. It was the closest he ever came to saying anything to a woman about his feelings: how he had watched her walking, stopping, squatting in a marsh by the river, how he'd seen her lips move. From a distance further than most hawks would bother screening the sky, Sunderd had watched her and wished he could touch her lips and cover them with his fingertips, stop her from saying something, something silly, as she looked up into his face to read his thoughts. . . .

If I was a horse, she said, tearing him from his dreams, I'd kick you.

In front of them, beside the ridge that tapered off to the beginning of a tree-line, a raven, looking gruff and bearded, hopped onto a fallen branch to watch them approach. Stiff and silent, the black bird waited there, as if for the right moment to disappear into the sky without being seen. And Sunderd, without knowing why, closed his eyes to let him.

*

The winter would be a cold one, Sera thought. The wind, already swirling in October, told her so. When she got home from the walk with Sunderd she unearthed the remaining carrots from her cache at the corner of the garden, and began canning whatever vegetables she had left over in large pickle jars in the basement. Then she had Pep bring home an empty wine barrel from the Legion. She grated the last of her frost-burnt cabbage and poured crystal salt into the barrel's mixture to make sauerkraut. She squeezed the juices to the top of the barrel with a wooden stamper and a heavy rock. After the cabbage had fermented for fourteen days she would bring it outside, by the back door. Within a week the sauerkraut would be settled enough for eating, and a week after that it would be frozen solid, she thought. For dinner, all they needed to do was take a chisel outside and break themselves off a block.

But it was in the basement, within the confines of damp shadows and mining picks, that her daily life left her for a time, and took her away from squeezing cabbage juice and bottling vegetables. Elbow-deep in salt water, her hands raw and wrinkled, Sera glimpsed, suddenly, a shape forming behind her that had no shadow, or a shadow that had no form.

It was just the same as in her dreams, something that didn't so much surprise her as confirm a feeling in her heart that someone had been there all along, growing quietly, like fate or mushrooms.

She wasn't afraid.

Without turning to look Sera thought she could see a woman's face and, barely, just the outline of her long coat trailing through a pile of Pep's tools. She thought she saw this out of the furthest corner of her eye: the woman's coat brushing through the shovels and picks without knocking them over, without breezing the air in the stagnant basement, *moving right through shovels and air.*

The woman didn't speak to her, of course, but Sera thought she might have been smiling while she watched her plunging her hands into the cabbage.

Hello, Sera said—as she said to all her dream people— and swivelled quickly, but the woman was gone, without leaving a word or scent to change the dampness in the room, and no amount of cabbage squeezing brought her back.

Sera hardly thought about the woman after that. She went right back to her work. The woman was one shadow, one dream, one flicker at the edge of Sera's sight among many, and among too many, lately, to count.

It could have been nothing at all.

In fact, Sera would have forgotten about her completely if she hadn't seen, upon leaving the basement, the trail her coat had made in the basement's dust. It appeared to have swung slightly from side to side, cleaning the floor as the woman walked. And the swipes or grooves that the coat left were like empty parentheses slashed into the floor, waiting to be filled.

Sera followed the parentheses up the wooden stairs, thinking of the hours she would have spent cleaning the same dust marks from the floor. Maybe not hours, but she might have done a more complete job of it, she thought, and cleaned more than just those marks. Two hours perhaps. It had taken that long to clean the steps when she'd first moved into the house, but she hadn't bothered to battle the dust since then, at least not to that extent. Twice, sometimes three times a day, Pep tracked coal from the basement to the kitchen stove.

The white marks went up the stairs, polishing each step, especially the edges where the woman's coat dragged over at a harsher angle, where they led her through Sera's kitchen and out to the front yard.

The parentheses ended there, in the middle of the yard, in the same spot where Sera had burned Pep's letters, eleven years before.

The woman's image meant little to Sera. She'd grown up hearing about ghosts. Her own brother had been so sick, her grandmother once told her, that they walked him into Reggio to be confirmed. On the way they saw two people walking toward them on the dirt path. Roma said they were about to nod hello when she recognized them as two girls who had recently died. The girls walked by them without seeing Sera's grandmother, brother and father, and when the family arrived at the church in Reggio, they were greeted, not by a priest, but by a cardinal. On the way back her father remembered a dream he'd had the night before and suddenly walked off the road, into the bush. Twenty paces from their path he picked up a rope that he said he knew would be there. He still has that rope, Roma told Sera, finishing the story and sending her away.

But whenever she told Sera this story Roma always seemed more amazed that a cardinal had baptized her brother than by the strange visions they had seen on the road. The old woman didn't tell her if that combination of events let her brother live, but Sera, from that day on, put cardinals in the same mental file as ghosts.

It wasn't a very exciting story, Sera thought later. But

then, most of them weren't; there just seemed to be more of those stories in Italy. She'd heard others recount stories of old uncles who died in the war, most often bachelors. One was bitten by his horse and died without actually fighting for Italy. He was said to appear by his sweetheart's favourite tree, leaving as soon as she waved to him. Another uncle once met a stranger from Germany, and spoke to him for two hours in perfect German, without ever having learned the language.

Even her brother had claimed to see a ghost, just after he'd fallen from a bergamot tree. He'd been night-fowling, he admitted, and the wind pulled him down from a bird's nest. The ghost, he said, tried to steal his breath.

When Sera remembered those stories she desperately wanted something like that to happen to her. When she started dreaming she knew that it could. The dead live in our dreams; her grandmother had told her that. Dreams can order the past more reliably than a remembrance. Dreams, Roma said, are the spirit of the past. They are what might have been. Still, a ghost who trailed clean spots along the floor was more of an embarrassment than a *ghost*. And Sera had no idea whose ghost it was.

*

Sauerkraut? For chrissakes, says Celi. Sera was Italian. Do you know any Italians who make sauerkraut? She might have made Christmas panettone, she might have made antipasto, she might have made a lot of things, wine even, but she sure as hell didn't make sauerkraut. *But the sauerkraut is incidental.*

*

Sunderd was busy that day. He was experimenting.

After moiling the morning away in *The History of*

African Medicine, he decided that he wouldn't even stitch his patients any more. He would avoid their insides. From now on they would be spread out on the ground, maybe in the thistles outside his underground shack, and treated there. They could watch crows, think about pine-cones digging into their shoulder-blades, do anything instead of worrying about what he was up to.

Ants, he said to himself, from now on I'll use ants.

The idea was a simple one, and the first miner to come to him with a cut forearm wasn't convinced that it would work.

Sunderd let him sit on a log by the fire pit. He had the miner—his name was Pep Rogolino—face the shed, to give him something to look at. Pep wasn't worried. He let Sunderd busy himself and waited on the log without looking at the horse. Pep had seen plenty of horses. The mine was full of them: Nugget, French, Dempsey, Charlie, Trixy, Jacks, Bullet, Bricks, Baldy, Mouse, Major, Buster, Ben, Dusty, Earl, Mickey, Fox, Stan, Pete, Prince, Silver, Top, Glen; one hundred and eight horses in all, pulling cars, corralled outside the mine during idle days, boiler scavenging, rock-dump pulling or just saddled up for errands and messages to town.

Sunderd's horse meant nothing more to Pep than all the others he'd worked beside. He regarded most of them with suspicion. They may plod through their tunnels, but come feeding time, horses could navigate the darkness with the grace of bats. If you saddled them up they bloated out their stomachs the same way, every time, trying to loosen the straps before lifting a hoof. And like most miners, they'd tell you they were working far harder than they were.

Sunderd disappeared for a moment, behind his shack, and Pep wondered if he'd run off for something. It sounded as though he was leaving, cutting through the woods and making for town. But he came back, quickly, materializing next to Pep with a fistful of black ants.

They should be bigger than this, Sunderd said, but it should work fine.

Pep flinched.

What the hell are you doing? I got a cut is all. Just stitch it up and I'll be on my way.

Pep had an aversion to doctors and medicine in general. He'd heard his mother, Teresa, call them the Mafia of the White Smock so often that her Old World skepticism had filtered into him and become his own. Organized crime, she'd said, and spent the last fifteen years of her life with a goitre on her neck, biting her thumb at any doctor who so much as whispered the idea that she could be fixed, good as new. The fifteen years that she'd outlived the doctors' advice proved her story true. It also gave Pep more fuel to conjure ideas on the subject of doctors: they name you sick so they can send you to their friend, the pharmacist, to buy pills. Never mind: it's all a racket.

And there was another story he knew, of a miner who had an arm paralysed by a doctor when an ordinary shot of cortisone hit a nerve. Pep visited him once in a while, but the arm hung down like a fresh-killed rabbit, or swung out of his pocket when the man turned suddenly, and its complete lifelessness put Pep off going there. He felt worse about not going over to see the man than he did about the man's injuries, but what could you do, he'd say to himself, it's that medicine that took his arm from him.

Perhaps Sunderd didn't count on Pep reacting badly. He might have thought that a couple of ants were harmless, weren't they? But then Sunderd remembered there were no bugs in the mines: that was the reason Pep was so jumpy.

I'm gonna stitch you with these, Sunderd said. New technique I've been reading about. He didn't add that it was from an article on South African soldier ants. Sunderd's reading material ranged widely; it wandered just as widely, in roving heaps throughout his shack, left beneath trees in the woods and forgotten on fence posts behind the whore-house.

All I have to do is line 'em up along the wound and the ants will squeeze it shut with their mouths.

Pep looked at him blankly while Sunderd rummaged through a worn-out handkerchief.

Pep opened his mouth. But no words came out.

Should take about three, maybe four ants, so hang on for a second and keep still. I don't reckon it will hurt at all. They're just going to pinch you is all. Then I'll snap off their heads.

Pep's throat was empty.

Yeah, this should work just dandy. Here's one sniffing around already. Wait a minute, don't move. You're making it bleed again. The ant can't pinch if he's swimming.

Sunderd smiled warmly despite seeing the blood. He wiped Pep's arm again, dabbing up the blood with a white cloth so his arm was clean and the cloth looked as if he'd painted a poppy, or a rose.

Shit mother! What the hell?

That was Pep speaking. His voice came back to him by the time Sunderd could put another ant on his arm. The first ant didn't seem to be working out quite right.

If his jaws were just a little bit bigger. . . .

I don't care how big his jaws are, an ant's not going to do it. Get a goddamn needle and thread the damn thing.

But Sunderd wouldn't hear of it:

Give him a minute more.

Sunderd said 'him' like the ant was more than an ant.

I've seen this work, in the latest medical journals. The ant will just pinch the edges and try for a bite, then I'll snip his neck and he'll stay there, just his head. You won't even have to come back to get stitches out. The head will just fall out.

Pep jumped up before Sunderd could root through his handkerchief for another ant. Sunderd swung around but

Pep was gone, running through the woods and breaking branches like a spooked horse.

God's stitches, Sunderd yelled. *Senti! Senti!* You could've been the first in the Pass with God's stitches!

*

I have to get moving, Fina says, his young voice suddenly screeching, echoing through the dark. A series of chirps and creaks fills their tunnel, crowding the mine's night with a thousand black birds. Then there are groans, from the timbers and from Celi. And one sentence: Just where in hell do you want to go? Celi puts his head down again, resting on his side. He thinks of where he could be now, right now: downtown in a bar. Maybe he and some buddies would make a run into Michel or the other direction to Blairmore for some off-sales. Maybe they'd stay there. The only men he would be taking care of would be his friends who fell down drunk in one bar, and had to be carried to the next and propped by the door. Somebody who'd been in the war called it 'carrying your dead', so when the men woke up they always repaid the favour by carrying the others home. Most times they had to, and somehow it worked out even. There was always an even number of corpses and men who could carry them, as if they'd planned it beforehand and taken shifts. Celi fights to think of something else. Instead of bar drinking he thinks about making wine. He finds that thought more relaxing. He thinks about the old way of making it, how he's seen his father leave the grape skins in the vats for a longer time than usual, to make his red wine especially dark. It was the skin, Celi remembers, that gave the wine its quality and flavour, even its colour. If his father took the skins away early enough the wine was white, a little later and it was a shade of pink, exactly like the wine from Ascoli Piceno. Longer still, after many more nights, the wine was deep scarlet, almost black, from Sardinia, he'd said. His father called the wine that evaporated from the top of its cask the angel's share. Whatever evaporated, vanished or disappeared wasn't mourned; it was payment for the magic to begin. There are other names Celi knows: a barrel of wine is called a *ferryman* in Noto, a *saint* in Etna. Celi lets his mind wander like this until he falls asleep again, and, for what seems like countless time, Celi starts to dream: *Sera*. She's in Pep's yard, their yard, coughing. Celi can hear the cough as plain as day, even in his dream. She reaches for her pocket and pulls out a small green frog and then, before Celi's eyes— he's watching, from a window—she puts the frog in her mouth. Celi thinks he sees a stray leg slip from her mouth but he's not sure. Before he can speak or move toward her, he sees Sera spit the frog out of her mouth. When it falls into her hand the frog tucks in its legs to gain a steady spot in her hand, and croaks. The frog, Celi can tell, now has Sera's cough. It goes on croaking, coughing more loudly than its little body would seem to allow, until Sera puts it back in her pocket and all Celi can hear is a muffled noise like somebody's stomach growling. Celi turns away and goes into the kitchen, looking for something to eat. But there is nothing. He looks everywhere. He looks in pots. He looks in drawers. He looks in the toaster to see if something is about to pop up, thinking: how can Sera eat that frog? How can he be so hungry after watching her? Celi is sure that she swallowed it. He is sure the frog went down her throat and came back out with whatever it was that made her cough, maybe the cold itself. Then Celi wakes up to the sound of groaning—his own stomach's groaning or the mine's groaning. (He listens for the difference, then he coughs.) There is a moment when the pebbled mattress that presses into his cheek is Sera's fingernails scratching their way across the night, a moment when he doesn't know where he is, or who he's with. And then he does. And she is gone. *Who is gone?*

*

It isn't the owner of the bottle who matters, but the contents within. The Bagnarote say the same phrase when railing against the land's owner, or the body's.

NINE

Maybe it was like this:

What else could Sunderd do? He was in love. Besides, the cut wasn't so bad that Pep couldn't walk into town. Any number of seamstresses or sailors could have sewn Pep's cut, tied a knot and sent him on his way. Sunderd merely wound him up and pointed him in the right direction. And why Pep came to him for such a simple job was another thing: didn't he know that Sunderd had been walking with Sera? Was he that much of a fool that he neither noticed nor cared what it might have led to? By the time the story made its way through the Pass it would be stretched a mile longer than it really was. Didn't Pep care?

All of these questions bothered Sunderd, more because he loaded the time he spent with Sera with so much significance. Their walks were practically the only social contact he had with another person. And they meant nothing to the one he secretly wanted to seduce and little to the other he wanted to piss off.

The whole thing was a mess, a mess from start to finish. For a brief moment he actually considered going into town himself and buying some booze. The way he felt, he'd probably pass Pep on the road. They would nod to each other and the game would be over. Pep would know that Sunderd was beaten and Sunderd would know that Pep knew all about his feelings for Sera; and this thought alone kept him from moving.

He sat outside his shack listening to his horse breathe. For a while he watched the remaining ants that he had freed climb over one of his boots and make their way across an ocean of crabgrass to the other boot. They clung to the leather. Each foot stuck, then released its grip.

Thinking about Sera made him tired of looking at ants, ravens and crows, tired of everything around him.

Sunderd stood up, kicking the dirt and ants from his boots. He went over to his barn—too small to be more than a shed—and looked over the half-door's ledge into the horse's eyes. The eyes were luminous orbs. The lids were half closed.

Sunderd opened the door and walked into the darkness of the shed. He was thinking of mounting her, something that he had never done before. The horse probably wasn't used to being ridden. He didn't even know if she'd done anything but pull cars of coal. He had a mind to find out, in fact he had a mental picture of himself with a sword on, mounting the horse from the left so that the sword would swing clear, Sunderd riding away to meet Sera. He imagined himself riding out of the woods, throwing himself down from the horse only when he reached her doorstep. Then he saw himself take Sera by her arm and lead her confidently into town, where he walked on the outside of the street to screen her from overhead chamber pots gushing from open windows. He thought of everything.

But the reality never made it to the first gallop. In his mind, Sunderd also pictured himself barely able to control the horse's reins. He saw himself most clearly swinging precariously from the horse's hams, or a leg perhaps, caught in the saddle's girth and hanging sideways to watch shit fall to the ground.

Sunderd was a man who knew his limitations. He prided himself on recognizing these limitations and cursed himself routinely for letting them hold him back from doing everything that he saw more foolish men attempt: swimming lakes, winning card games, eating twenty pies. It wasn't that he thought he could achieve those things if he tried them, or that he wanted to try them; it was in the trying.

For a fleeting moment he wanted to try everything.

For Sunderd, everything was, necessarily, Sera.

*

Pep, of course, didn't know anything was happening with Sera and Sunderd. To be fair, Sera didn't know anything was happening with Sera and Sunderd. Life was running along the same smooth rails it always had for Pep, as if his fate was steady and solid, running on clear, even tracks. If he switched rails it was with the gentle and fluid motion a guitar player uses to slip his fingers down from one key to another.

He had fixed his arm in town, just as Sunderd had predicted. The ant story would make some lively conversation in the wash-house, or later in the bar. Pep shook his head when he thought of it, the same incredulous wag of his head that he would make a week later when he found his house empty of Sera, empty even of her skin's scent, the whole of her evaporated.

*

Now, thirty-five years later, more than just Sera had disappeared from his house. Most of her changes were gone too. Once again, there were no lampshades on the bulbs, so moving around the house from one patch of light to another was like being a moth, bulb-driven. Life was the same as before she blew through.

Some people, she'd said, *are so open, the wind just seems to blow right through them*.

But no wind blew through his house. Pep had built the

basement (if it's possible to build a hole) after the house, so the only odour there was came from the earth. The basement's dampness was an old man's smell, or perhaps it suited an old man.

The basement floor was a layer of dirt, hardened by water leaks and thousands of footsteps. The concrete walls were left almost exactly as they were when they'd first dried. Two-by-four ridges lined the walls right to the basement's ceiling, or to the kitchen's floor-boards. But all Sera's canning was gone.

There were some additions, though: a brand-new furnace, hardly used because Pep preferred the dry heat from his coal stove. A pile of web-ridden shovels, thrown down as soon as the digging was finished. An assortment of cardboard, pails, rolls of tin, axes and mining picks. There were hammers, huge hammers meant for railway spikes. Leftover pieces of oddly shaped wood, some of it driftwood (from where?), some half sawn and abandoned, carelessly thrown into a spiky pile that would have reached Pep's chest. Broken chairs, paper bags full of screws, stacks of *National Geographics*, curtains, blankets, bottles and wooden casks that would rival a Roman catacomb full of Amontillado. And there were boxes: cardboard boxes filled with local newspapers dating as far back as 1910, electrical manuals and the like.

Sunderd's underground shack was far different. Except for one shovel, there wasn't a tool to be found. In place of bottles, he left books, many books. Most were eighty-year-old medical texts that linked automobiling with sexual impotence:

> There is an inclination in some quarters to make
> fun of von Notthafft's claim that automobiling
> speed mania is apt to result in sexual impotence.
> He has had five such cases in his own practice—
> four of the patients were rich men, while the fifth
> was a chauffeur. . . .

The books contained chapters entitled: "A Story without a Moral"; "The Price of a Kiss"; "Peculiar, but Absolutely True"; "Imprisonment for a Kind Act"; "A Topsy-Turvy World"; "What Would You Have Told Him?"; "Pollutions or Wet Dreams"; "The Solitary Vice"; "On the Use of Perfume"; "The Limitation of Offspring"; and "Should Venereal Disease Be Reported?" There were physicians' recipes for treating freckles with grated horse-radish and buttermilk; reversing hair loss with boiled rosemary leaves, coconut oil and a few drops of verbena; removing gunpowder facial stains with mixtures of ammonium, distilled water and diluted hydrochloric acid; reducing a big nose by sleeping with a brace that compressed the artery that supplied the nose; preventing insomnia by eating an apple and sleeping near a large bowl of water; relieving rheumatism by chewing dried rhubarb roots in a sulphur spring (if possible) and applying mustard-oil externally after the bath.

But there were more: boxes of mail-order books, pamphlet chapter-books really, on every subject conceivable. *The Crime of Superstition*; *Masterpieces of Erotic Literature*; *A Book of Rogues and Impostors: A Historical and Critical Summary of Legends, Swindles, Hoaxes and Rackets*; *Advice to the Lonely*; *How Comic Strips Are Made*; *Amazing Confessions*; *A Guide to American Spas, Mineral Springs and Watering Places*; *The Evolution of the Virtue of Chastity*; *The Pope and the Italian Jackal: How Mussolini's Invincible Legions Were Blessed*; *Sexual Osphresiology*; *The Evolution of Property*; *The Next Fifty Years: 1950—1999*; *The Story of the World's Oldest Profession*; *The One-Shot Cure for Syphilis and Gonorrhea, Including Some Angles the Professors and Moralists Have Over-Looked*; *The Right to Be Lazy and Other Studies*; *The Sexual History of the War*; *Making Paper Airplanes*; *The Torch of Life*; *The Atheism of Astronomy*; *English Etymology*; *Power to Love*; *The Miraculous Revenge*; *Love Tales of Italian Life*; *How Man Made God*; *Memory: What*

It Is and How to Use It; *The End of the World*; *Nicholas and Alexandra*; *Darwin and the Theory of Evolution*.

There were hundreds more.

After Sera left, Sunderd abandoned the books and his solitude. He moved back to town. Pep, on the other hand, escaped to the pub, and after that, in the evenings, he sat at his kitchen table. He wasn't a man who liked to sit in a lone chair beneath a tree. He didn't watch the traffic, except in a bar, with his back securely against a wall. And when he went out, he seemed suspicious of most everyone he met. His eyes narrowed. The crow's-feet beside his eyes shrank smaller and tighter, imprints made, perhaps, by more dainty birds than scavengers. But he looked scavenged none the less. He'd lost any gentleness he had in his youth.

His forehead was smooth, impossibly smooth for such an old man, and his cheeks had a façade of sated warmth that seemed like a smile without him making one. That was good, because he didn't so much smile as he shook his head to shrug his thoughts away.

If he was tired this morning, before he went to the mine, he didn't admit it.

Talking came easier with the legs bent, he said, sitting on the café's only hard-backed chair. Sera, he might have added, never said much because she was always moving about, awake or asleep. You could hear her clacking away with those slippers all day long if you wanted to—even after she left. But she kept to herself mostly. As Pep did now.

All this was revealed only in the shrug he gave his listener, the waitress, when he shook his head so slightly it was more of a shiver.

But who the hell could tell you what goes on in a woman's head?

*

The man who comes to Bagnara and gives up his secrets grudgingly can never be cleansed from an unlucky past. He holds onto his fate. He carries it like his death and takes it wherever he goes.

The honest man, however, lets himself be not only shaved but skinned. These men come to Bagnara the same way they sit down in a chair, hold out their necks and tell a story to a barber. They are the lucky ones. They understand that ill fortune and drops of olive oil only spread with time. They believe that what might have happened in their past is more important than what did happen. And they know that they can be freed from their past, as from their whiskers. The tales that they tell the women can be real, supposed or imagined, but at the very least, they must be told. So they come to Bagnara with open hearts and clean, exposed necks.

C'era una volta, an older Celi wasn't sleeping in a mine. He was under a fig tree. He'd chosen that tree because he knew that fig trees brought joy and good health. Fig trees increased mother's milk, the barren became pregnant and the thin became stout. He'd shied away from a walnut tree, the tree of witches, a tree that only brought sorrows, until he couldn't even see it from where he'd sat down. With his head resting against the fig's trunk, his last sight was a blackbird, high in the branches above him, sharpening its beak against the tree's skin.

And then Celi fell asleep. He saw a thin woman in mourning clothes, a black scarf wrapped around her hair, walking toward him on the path that led back to Scilla. The woman was kind-looking, and because she was alone, he nodded his head to her as they passed. The woman nodded back.

A month later they were married. Celi raised her two sons as his own, while respecting the empty void that their dead father had left with them. A woman and her mother-in-law were like two knives in the same sheath, but two men in one house was far worse, so Celi honoured their father's memory. He might have brought the boys into his house, but he praised them in their own right. They were a happy family, he thought, and there was just enough room for the four of them—five, if you counted their father's unspoken memory.

His new wife brought him much more than happiness. She surprised him with a different meal almost every day of their life together. Even the bread changed at every sitting: spongy loaves of *muffelettu,* double-rolled *cucchia, turticedda* and *panettone* cakes, artichoke *cacociula, scalitedda* ladders, *cucciddatu* rings, *ciuriddu* flowers, cross-shaped *pani di morti, minnuzzi* breasts, eyeglasses, crooked *ciumi tortu* rivers, ox-feet, *pagnotta* buns and *ciabatta* slippers. The breads she made were both local specialities and from more distant kitchens. The slippers, she said, were left in Messina by Spanish conquerors. If you went to Madrid you would see the same shape of bread, even today, but nowhere else besides Sicily. The Greeks, the French, the Portuguese: they all left bits of language and bread in Italy, it seemed, and all of it found its way to Celi's table. His wife made him a new kind of bread no matter how much he said that he'd enjoyed the last one. Some days he wondered if she could make the same bread twice. Later, Celi decided that she liked to surprise him, and that many of the breads were in fact her own creations. It just wasn't possible that so many slippers, hats, rings, fingers, flowers, eyeglasses and ladders had been left behind in Sicily and Calabria.

But he never questioned her ability. He'd seen how some husbands ran their houses. They could turn their wives into silent files who ground through the day, as through their marriage, and Celi was old enough to know better. From the moment they were married, the kitchen, the house and all its functions became hers alone to steady.

When she died the next winter, Celi continued his unspoken promise to the two boys. He took care of them and saw to their education. The five of them continued on, somehow, despite the strangeness of their household. At the end of ten years, her two sons were grown and they left Celi's house to find America. He said goodbye to them in Reggio di Calabria with a long, sober face. Then he walked home, to his city of house-bridges, to find his own house unbearably empty.

Celi woke up with tears and clouds in his eyes. When he brushed them from his face he saw that the blackbird was still in the fig tree above him, watching him.

He couldn't sleep for two nights afterward. The dream disturbed him so much that he couldn't rid himself of his emptiness. Finally, on the third day, he decided to visit a Bagnarota. Celi walked into Bagnara by himself, in the early evening. There was no moon. A light at the end of the street guided him to a house he'd heard other men describe in drunken moments. The woman who answered the door said she'd been waiting for him, and he'd hardly finished his story when she pushed him down to the floor, hiked up her seven skirts and peed on him. The map she drew across his shirt spread to his hips and warmed the small of his back.

Her legs were hairy but that was the most that he could bear to look at. Truthfully, he'd fixed his eyes on a leg of prosciutto—peppercorned and cured—that was hanging near the fireplace, so perhaps he was mistaken. She was also finished so quickly that it astonished him.

You're clean now, she said, much to his relief. He wanted to ask about the dream but she answered that question before he asked it: The dead live in dreams. You can forget the past or you can chase it. Whatever you decide, that is your fate. Now get out of my house.

Celi took her advice. He went home. He changed into new clothes. The house felt better to him, even though his dream-family's memory was still fresh in his mind. They were now four shapes without substance.

He couldn't help looking for some trace of them. The Bagnarota had all but told him to search for their memory, as futile as that seemed. So Celi looked everywhere, into every photo, pocket and handkerchief he could find. Not a sign remained from his dream. It was only later, the next day, that he did find something, finally. In probably the last place he could look, on the corner-most shingle of his house, pointing toward Sicily, he found a bird's nest.

Two young blackbirds looked up at him from the nest, and Celi took care of them, feeding them bread crumbs, until they were strong enough to fly away.

*

Sunderd wasn't ready to see Sera.

That day he'd paced around his hole in the woods for an hour or two, ploughing his feet through fallen leaves and dried pine needles. Then he'd walked into town, taken a sulphur bath at the Sanatorium and felt better for it. His solitary life was miles away.

Still, walking through the slide's wreckage, he must have felt queasy. The mile of grey, fallen rocks jutted out of the ground too sharply not to enter his thoughts. His hair was wet and slicked back. There was a slight breeze that made his ears cold and red, not from the sulphur's warmth, but from the wind's bite. Normally, he would have waited at the San until his hair was dry, but something had told him to get moving.

And now, when he saw her, all he could think was that he wasn't ready. Not yet.

He'd never had the courage to meet Sera any other way than by chance, but he'd also never figured out exactly how to control that chance once it came to him. Every time he saw her he felt as though he needed to find a chair to push away from himself, just to gain some momentum. And every time he told himself there'd been enough puttering around.

Today, he said to himself. It will be today.

Incredibly, it was.

When he saw Sera rounding the side of the road toward Turtle Mountain he decided to follow her until he thought of something to say. He walked fifty feet behind her, watching her skirt sway a little as she moved. When she turned off the road, on the other side of the rocks, he saw she was heading for the mine. Sunderd quickened his pace.

He caught up to her just inside the yard, faster than he'd planned. The mine was closed, he saw. Nobody but Sera was in the compound. A strike, he remembered, had shut everything down until somebody got enough money to close an eye to the lack of safety. He didn't know who.

Sunderd could see she hadn't slept soundly for many nights, if she'd slept at all.

Her eyes, he told her, were like two in the snow. He didn't say, 'two piss holes', but the joke seemed clear enough. He meant to chide her gently, a word or two to bring her back to herself, if only to make her smooth pallor crack a smile. He felt he knew her well enough to add: Hey, you better get to bed before you meet yourself getting up. But he stopped short of finishing the sentence when she didn't look at him.

Sera didn't register anything he'd said. She glided quietly past him, walking softly past the wash-house, past Sunderd's trailing voice. She moved smoothly through the tipple's thick shadow, all the way to the mine entrance, where she emerged, finally, under the tunnel's concrete frame. The date of the mine's opening, 1908, was engraved into the stone above her. Sera stood there and leaned toward the darkness, slightly under the eight. Sunderd would have gone after her if she'd gone into the tunnel but she seemed only curious. She was listening, he thought, to the flow of air coming out. The other air tunnel was open and pushing clean air into the mine, even while the mine was closed for the strike.

Sunderd waited beside the tipple, both wishing Sera

would turn around and hoping she wouldn't. He looked around for something to do with his hands, or someplace to go besides after her. The nearest door was locked, as he might have guessed if he'd been thinking about it. The lamps were stored there, all of them checked, cleaned and refilled for the next shift. The next building was the wash-house. He went past the first door—which led to his sinks and the showers—and stopped at the door where the miners usually exited. Somehow he knew it would be open even before he tried the handle. A bench or two and some large clothes-hooks didn't need to be bolted down.

Without people the room was so bare Sunderd hardly recognized it. The hooks were empty; most were near the ceiling, clawing at nothing but his memories. The ropes were fastened to the floor, to the walls, tied to black iron rings. There were some lockers against the far wall, but the hooks held his attention the longest. They were either small anchors or huge lures, strung completely across the ceiling. As he walked under the hooks, stepping around their lines, trying not to entangle himself, Sunderd caught himself holding his breath.

The only window was in the other room, near his sinks.

*

When the North Wind plucked her geese and sent the first flurries to the Pass, Sunderd would fight the wind for as long as he could. As he walked he pushed against her, bent over like a candle, his face white and wet, his back warm and dry. And the people he met along the roads, from Frank to Coleman, did the same. They warred with the wind, bending one way or another. Those who walked backwards saved their faces and let the wind and snow assail their backs. Half-ghosts like Sunderd walked with an arm in front of their faces, squinting their white lashes.

But when Sera walked away from him, making her way past the wash-house, Sunderd thought about quite a different kind of ghost.

He'd once lit a match and watched the first puff of smoke lift itself from the matchstick still in his fingers. He'd seen the puff spread out in a single white ring; it rose and grew into a circle the size of his fist. And just when he started to stumble backward, the circle of smoke tilted slightly toward him, facing him, and instantly disappeared. Sunderd was filled with the most extraordinary sense of calmness and hope. He couldn't remember feeling such hope before that day. Later, when he thought about the ring at odd moments—no more than a handful of times over the years—he felt the same flicker of wonderment. Each time he dismissed it from his thoughts as quickly as the smoke had vanished from his eyes. And if asked about ghosts, souls, fate, God or the dead miners that came to see him after a blast, he dismissed those questions in the same way: respectfully . . . just in case.

But she was haunted, he thought. Sera looked exactly like someone who was haunted.

Sunderd watched her for a while—from the other room. He watched her from the only window in the wash-house, its glass dirty and wind-scrawled with coal dust, letting his breath moisten the surface enough to make him want to clean it. But he left the window as it was, a white flower of moisture appearing and disappearing just under his line of vision. The dust on the glass screened him somewhat if she happened to turn back.

But she didn't. She stood quietly under the mine's entrance, as if she were waiting for a bus to come out and stop for her. If not a bus, then something else would come out of the mountain, but whatever it was, it would be expected. Man, horse or butterfly, Sera would be there to greet it. Sunderd knew this.

The entrance was big enough for most anything to come

out. Its tunnel was as wide as a house, with two sets of railway tracks that ran to the right, arcing out of the mine toward the tipple.

When she walked to the left of the entrance and made her way up the hill, Sunderd was more disappointed than she could have been. Or perhaps she had expected nothing to come out of the mine, and it had. Whatever had happened, she disappeared into the bush, her red jacket blending with the rough, brown colours of fall.

Sunderd turned from the window.

He remembered his work in this building, like the work itself, in pieces. He'd patched men together, or straightened them out, tying their jaws shut with strings that resembled slingshots, fastening the lines in careful knots behind the miners' heads. Their chins rested like walnuts in the slings. Their arms were tied together, resting across their stomachs, as were their legs, to stop their hips from splaying out.

It wasn't just for the coffins' sake Sunderd did that; sometimes the men jerked or moved around if he didn't tie them down properly. They could do that, hours afterward, he remembered. They could twitch, shudder even, as if from a dream, fall off the edge of a table and almost wake up, cursing him for not tying better knots.

So the apologies he wove together were just as cautious, just as intricate as the bonds that held them in their world. There wasn't anything else he could have done, or said.

*

Sera pushed herself up from the ground. She was tired now.

She left the mine's hillside, twenty yards above the entrance, and started walking down with the idea of waving goodbye to Sunderd on her way past. He was still inside the wash-house, probably—at least she hadn't noticed him leave. But she wasn't entirely sure that she would have noticed anything that happened around her. The day-dreaming washed her out of her more immediate surroundings. It left her slightly dazed and foggy, her thoughts broom-swept: clean but scratched. Nothing was ever entirely clear and everything in the dream's way was pushed aside or forgotten, like the arm that buried her head and begged a dream to visit her. Sometimes a dream came to her when she tried to imagine the air that hung in front of what she was looking for and the thing that was always looking for her, that other self, her dream self. But today it hadn't worked. She couldn't see the air in between. She couldn't move from the day to the living shadows of her past.

*

Everybody stretched it there a mile long, says Celi. Sure she went walking. She may have seen things, too. But stories like that get spread by every gossip-monger in the Pass. They aren't real. (A timber groans, cutting through the space between Celi and Fina. The sound changes into a high, wooden chirp, making Celi look up for the dark bird somewhere above him.) *There are people living in hilltop towns, in the north of Italy, who see the sun setting against the Dolomites every evening. They see the trees that wash up their mountainside turning from green to red, and they still say the little men are busy painting.* You don't believe that too, do you? *They don't believe it. They just say it. It's a story.* That's exactly what these are for chrissakes, what more do you want? Celi feels pale, and weak. His stomach again, he thinks. He is tired of talking to Fina, so even the darkness can't dull the sharp edge of his words. You don't know shit, he thinks to himself. A bucker. What does a bucker know about anything? Celi stretches his arms, settles back on a blanket of rocks. He hears a dripping noise beside him and crosses his fingers together on top of his chest. He bends his fingers, slowly, only at the middle knuckles, so that they are a concave roof covering his navel from rain. He could almost sleep, he thinks. (But the gap between two long creaks brings him back.) The thing you got to know is, that guy, that guy Pep, used to have a mean streak in him from asshole to breakfast. I suppose his father gave it to him. The old man Rogolino— what the hell was his name—Francesco, I think. *Francesco.* That's right, that's right. Only they didn't call him that mostly. I heard they called him just Ciccio for short. Or the Turk. He was dark, that guy. He had dark skin. But then most of those southern Italians are dark, part African if you ask me. Some people say that Garibaldi didn't unite Italy; he divided Africa. Everything below Rome is, and always was, a hundred years behind the rest of the world. Calabria is no different. Anyway, that Ciccio could drink. Not like some guys mind you. Two beers and he'd get on a crying jag, tears all over the bloody place, and then he'd fall asleep. Finally died in a snowbank on the way home from a card game. Just tucked himself in a blanket of snow like he didn't want anybody disturbing him and froze to death a block from his front porch. They used to play low-ball poker back then. Five cards, lowest hand wins. Every hand plays and the house rakes off the pot, not much, but enough, including what the town gets and the Mounties. It was illegal, you know, but everybody knew about it. You just had to spread the money around to the right people. Pep was different though. Used to drink and get mad. Not even a crow could fly over his land, his house, or his head for that matter, after he'd been drinking, or he'd run into the house for the gun and started shooting at the sky. Later it was clouds—used to wait around all afternoon for just the right elephant to float over his head, like he was waiting in the bush for a flock of mallards. Christ, it's a good thing he mostly got drunk at night when he couldn't see half the clouds he wanted to wait around for. Sometimes he shot at the sun, but this all happened after Sera left. He drank for a while, that's for sure. Quit the mine and walked around like he'd been in a blast or something. They do that, those guys who come out of a blast. They all do that. Anyway, that's why I think Pep took to the bottle so easily. He inherited Ciccio's weakness for booze, not the crying, mind you, but a weakness just the same: enough to tell you whose pecker he came from. He was alone, what the hell. He loved her, make sure you get that straight right now. He really loved Sera. And she up and left. She disappeared. But I'll tell you, she wasn't the first one to do that. A lot of women didn't like it here, couldn't stand the Pass. That wasn't too damned strange. They'd left their families. They left everything, came here for a better life and found a pile of rocks. It was tough back then. Some of them went right back to Italy, Slovenia or wherever the hell they came from and some of the proud ones just hung themselves slow-like from a hook in their outhouse. That wasn't too bloody strange neither you know. When we get out, go check for yourself. The records are all there, in the town hall, or the graveyard for that matter. Go have a look. All the really big tombstones for women, with the twisty iron gates all around them, are just the ones I'm talking about. They have fancy holders for the flower wreaths, wrought iron that's ordered straight from Pittsburgh, pink marble from Verona, everything, the whole hog. Sera didn't have a funeral. Pep just dug the damned thing to have a place to go and look at her name I guess. Most people figured she got tired and run off. Like I was saying, a lot of them left, one way or another. Sera left too, in her own way. The same way some crazy man brings all his enemies into one room, tells them he's going to kill them all, then shoots himself. For him, they are dead, aren't they? She wanted the Pass to disappear, and for her, it did. In fact, it's still disappearing. There isn't much left really. Most of the people still here say that she left and met a man or she left and met a bear. Same ending: she left. Pep dug a hole. Hey, anybody who was smart didn't walk around the bush at night, with or without a hunting jacket. But even the stupid ones who had at least a little bit in their *cocuzza* carried some salt pork with them to throw at the bears. I heard Sera did that, but who knows? A nice sack of pork might have bought her some running time. Most of the trail blazers carried it when they were looking for new mines, guys like Giovanni Veltri. Did you know that? (Fina doesn't answer.) No, no, there's a lot you don't know yet. A lot you'll never know.

*

There were happier times for Sunderd to remember. He'd taken miners out of better places than coal-mines. When the parents were living wherever they could, he usually took them from chicken coops—babies more hatched than born. Some of the parents, being new immigrants, were that threadbare. They couldn't afford to rent rooms. At a loss for baby clothes, Sunderd wrapped more than one future miner in sheets of cotton gauze, bundling them up into little ghosts for their new Canadian fathers.

Once, when he couldn't find a warm place for the new miner, he turned off their stove, put the baby in a pot, and put the pot in the stove. He was the Biscuit Boy, they said, kept warm in the best cradle Sunderd could find.

These were the memories he fought to stitch together in his mind, trying to forget the cold miners they inevitably became. Even if they lived through those blasts they always emerged from the tunnels more cold than warm. Something happened to them while they waited in the dark, something far different from just a long shift in the mine. When they were rescued they all seemed to keep to themselves, exactly the opposite of what Sunderd expected them to do. They kept busy, working on chores, hardly talking to others. He didn't know why they did that, but he thought he'd felt the same kind of loneliness, the same need to keep moving, without explanation. More than once he had run from his own shadow.

Most of all he ran from the shadow that the wash-house had cast over his life. Just being in the room stirred more than he could handle, more images than he could possibly weave into a unified whole. They were so convoluted, so haphazardly sewn together, that he felt he'd created a monster of memory, one that he couldn't possibly bury, or perhaps hadn't buried completely. Too many of those memories were connected, the ugly ones he'd rather forget and the good ones he desperately wished to grasp and call his own. When he'd moved out to his shack in the woods he might have escaped the mine but he'd lost something too. He'd abandoned something distinctly human.

*

On the way back, she passed his wash-house twice. The first time Sera simply walked by his window, with the same gentle sway that pushed her hips from side to side like an axe through his heart, without glancing in his direction. Her green skirt rippled slightly as she walked, as she blew by his window the same way he'd seen her walk toward the mine entrance. Her feet barely stirred the dust.

The second time she nodded, pushing a faint smile toward him. He hadn't seen her return. Yet both times she was walking away from the mountain. Both times she was walking toward Sunderd, as if there were two Seras coming down from the hill, moving past the mine and his wash-house. It was growing dark, he thought; she might have doubled back. But this rationale didn't help him as much as it should have.

When he opened the door and called her name, the second Sera turned.

I can help you, he wanted to say. I think I can help you.

With what he didn't know. Sunderd wasn't sure if she was searching for something or trying to leave something behind. But he had experience with both, he wanted to say. He knew them both.

She was walking back toward him, steadily, before he could think of what to say. She walked into him and pushed him back so that he almost tripped, catching himself against the sink.

She was against his body then, hugging him, his right hand still on the edge of the sink, his left hanging numbly by his side. She squeezed him hard, pushing him back, making him start to slide over the sink's edge. He felt his legs spread to accommodate her body and stop himself from being pushed right into the sink. Then her hands were around him, hinged to his belt or his shirt, and he was being pulled toward her. When his legs came back to the floor his feet straddled her body.

Her mouth slipped across his cheek and down to his throat, digging into his neck as his left hand came to life and slid across her lower back. He didn't know what she wanted him to do but she froze then and let him touch her. Sunderd suddenly wanted to touch her everywhere at once, with his hands, with his lips. He wanted to put his palm flat against her chest, between her breasts, just to reassure himself that she was somewhere inside.

The thought surprised him.

But his elbows couldn't bend enough when she stood so close to him. He could touch only her back and the sides of her breasts, his thumbs anxiously shifting, tracing under her armpits, down her ribs.

She didn't move to free his hands, but kept hugging him, completely still. When he plied his right hand between his stomach and hers he could just touch her bare skin with the back of his hand. One of his knuckles slid into her navel.

When she turned around quickly she threw her head back. His nose was safely out of the way but she almost pushed him into the sink. Sunderd grabbed her shoulders to steady himself as Sera leaned back against him, with her arms folded across her stomach. He wanted to unbutton her blouse but he was suddenly unsure of what his hands should be doing.

Standing behind her, Sunderd could only look over her shoulder at the open door. The mine and the mountain were just twenty yards away. The sink that he was leaning against was cold and made him shiver. He wanted to leave.

But another push sent her away from him, winding him slightly. Without looking back, she walked toward the door.

Sunderd regained his balance and stepped forward suddenly, thinking all at once: she's going to leave. His head was throbbing.

But she didn't leave. Sera stopped moving a foot from the entrance, and reached for the door's edge. She made as if to close the door, but seemed to change her mind. Her back to him, she swung the door three-quarters open. Sunderd couldn't see what she was looking at. She was blocking most of the doorway. And without seeing her face, he couldn't begin to read what she was thinking.

The trees to the base of the mountain were a light brown, despite being evergreens, and the mountain's shade washed their colour away from what would normally have made a gentle green slope. In the evening light the trees were painted red. The path toward the mine entrance was smooth and flat, like a shadow that funnelled into darkness.

It was sunset, though the mountains hid the sun.

And the wind—there was always a wind—must have felt cold against her skin.

TEN

She walked around. She kept to herself. Then she disappeared. That's what happened. Why do you have to look further than that? (The mine answers for Fina, dropping what Celi thinks is cap rock falling to the floor. It sounds deep, perhaps a level or two below them. But the rocks drop almost rhythmically. He listens for a time before speaking again.) She may have dreamed about Italy before she disappeared, but what the hell does that matter? She buggered off. A lot of them left. They go back to where they came from or they stay here forever. Look at Pep: he'll never leave. Those guys who walk out of the mine never get out of the Pass. They walk around just like Sera used to, I guess.

*

The whole time she thought about how the Bagnarote were said to pee on men. For a price, they could shed misfortune from a man and cleanse him from his past. *If you are unlucky you must go to Bagnara*, Roma had told her. The women in Bagnara knew what to do with a man who was unlucky, who was ill-fated.

But the men who went there always wore their oldest clothes, Roma said, a poor sign, from the start. If you want to take off misfortune you must wear the clothes you wear every day. Wearing any other clothes will shed someone else's *sfortuna*, maybe someone from your past who doesn't really need it, she'd said. It was like picking up a comb that didn't belong to you and being made to straighten paths you would not have taken, or paths that you had travelled and straightened already.

Sera felt as though she'd picked up a comb, or was shedding someone else's misfortune, though in fact she was the one on top of Sunderd, rasping her body against his, shedding herself from herself.

She took him quickly, almost too quickly, mashing him against the floor with all her weight, then falling down on his chest—his shirt still on—and burying his face between her two breasts. She arched her back to her own rhythm, ignoring Sunderd's little movements or struggles for breath, as if it didn't matter if he was inside her or not.

Most of the time he wasn't.

She locked her elbows tightly against his shoulders, scrunching his whole body thin with her arms and thighs, her breasts now swallowing his face, her whiteness enveloping him, smothering him, until he completely disappeared, or tried to, burrowing deeper. She stayed like that, her body's rhythm against his gradually slowing down, then hardly moving, but focusing on every twitch of him, inside her, as she ground herself to a full, and final, stop.

In those last seconds the room became still, as if she couldn't hear anything, or perhaps there hadn't been a sound. She didn't remember making one.

But when the sound of her breath and the wind whistling through the next room's open door came back to her, she pushed herself up on one elbow and Sunderd, panting, fell out of her. He almost tumbled out.

Sera raised herself up over him and kissed him—for the first time—on the lips.

ELEVEN

I hear a horse. Do you hear that? It's nothing. They don't bring horses this far. I told you: the coal gets shovelled down the chutes from here. And the sound carries for a while. (They listen to the darkness.) Celi hears the timbers playing against each other. He hears falling cap rock. The creaking is there too, and the invisible currents of methane roping through the tunnel, twisting their knots tight. There is also the unmistakable sound of birds screeching through the mine-shaft and horse's hoofs clacking against the hard rock floor. But Celi doesn't say anything. He is no longer answering Fina, preferring to wash in and out of the tunnel's storied darkness without argument. He seems deepest in the mine when he leaves Fina's questions, but he can't help it. Celi can't understand why they haven't come yet. The next shift must have started by now. He thinks about Pep seeing the missing tags. Pep will see the bucker's first. If he's sharp Pep will look over to the other rack, the one they keep for extra work. Then he'll send somebody strong to carry them out, in case they need it: somebody like O'Shea, or Buster. Men like that dig pits with shovels twice the normal size in half the time. With one hand gripping the leg of a stool they can lift a man right into the air. Those men have hands the size and shape of cleavers. They carry even the widow-maker, fully assembled, on their shoulders like a floor mop. The widow-maker looks like an iron machine-gun and drills holes into rock and coal that can later be filled with sticks of dynamite. They never blow that kind of charge next to methane, but Celi knows some of the miners who've done it in other places. The dust from the drill sends most of them into early retirement, which accounts for its name and in part why Celi never operates the machine. He isn't so much afraid of the machine as he is too slight to operate it and make rock into dust. The man who drills needs to stand behind the gun, with all his weight, even after it is screwed into floor, ceiling and walls by iron rods. He needs to push it into the rock while dust sprays across his face. If he's strong enough, like Buster, he can cart it around without taking the damn thing apart, and that saves time. It means more coal for the whole shift. The only time those guys get into any trouble with the machine is when they carry the widow-maker up a ladder and the rungs break under their feet. Buster himself is heavy enough to break most ladders. Pep should have sent him here by now.

*

They'd gone further into the wash-house, under the hooks. Sunderd didn't feel comfortable next to the sinks and he wanted to get away from the open door, the mountain and the window that faced it. But looking up at the ceiling, at the anchors, with his back stuck to the cold, bare floor, Sunderd felt more shipwrecked than anything else. He spread his shirt out on the floor and even that seemed to wash away from him. In the end he tried to escape the room by hiding his head between her breasts.

But in the corners of his vision he could just make out the lines that were attached to the clothes-hooks. They were pulled taut and seemed to keep the ceiling above them. From the floor, the whole wash-house was made of lines, of rope. When he drew himself up, further into her warmth, he could completely disappear from the room.

Afterward, even without Sera on top of him, Sunderd felt

he'd escaped. His shirt was rumpled and wet with sweat but he tugged at the sides to make it snug across his back and shoulder-blades. His hands moved quickly up the buttons— he'd lost one—to his collar. He flapped his blue checkered tie back around his neck within seconds. The tie was too dull to be gaudy, but he didn't mind. He was enjoying their moment together and their silence. His hands made the tie's knot quickly, more of a well-versed benediction, while Sera stood next to a bench, at the edge of the room, watching him, her blouse open.

She smiled and Sunderd smiled back.

When he bent to pull up his pants, she said thank you, the first words she had spoken. Then she left.

Sera grabbed her jacket off the floor and blew out of the wash-house just as quickly as she'd come in, closing the door behind her.

Sunderd went to the window in the other room and saw her walking away from him, past the lamp-house. When Sera turned the corner to leave the mine site he lost sight of her.

He brought his left hand up to his nose to smell her but that too was gone. The floor, its dust and all the ancient grit from a miners' wash-house clouded whatever bits of Sera had stuck to his skin. But suddenly all of those things didn't matter.

Sunderd turned from the window and walked over to the nearest sink. He picked up a bar of soap and, without hurrying, washed his hands under a cool stream of water.

*

Facing the wind, Sera pushed herself away from the wash-house. The wind was stronger now, especially when she left the sides of the mine buildings, which could fight the wind better than she could. She zipped her jacket up and hugged herself as she walked. Two miles later, after she thrust herself into the dusty grey town, past false-fronted buildings, cottages, mercantile companies, community and miners' halls, past graveyards more known for their mass burials and long trenches than for individual memorials, past the square wooden church and the Sanatorium, past the brick whorehouse, past the wooden Chinese restaurant, past the wooden ceramic store and the whole wooden world, she started to cry.

It was the first time she'd cried during her walks, the first time the wind had licked the salt from her eyes before she could taste it. And it was the first time she screamed into the wind and felt it scream back, the wail coursing through her hair like fingers that slipped over her forehead and ran along her scalp. The wind's fingers blew down her neck and bunched into fists, bubbling out her blouse and jacket behind her arms and back. As she bent her body more into the wind, pushing harder against the wailing, the fists ballooned into a large sack behind her, like a heavy pillow that seemed to weigh her down as she walked.

When she got home Pep had already eaten. He'd made himself a sandwich, or something toasted, by the looks of it. The crumbs were left on the counter, his plate by the side of the sink. It wasn't a message for her. Pep was used to her walking about, not usually so late, but he was used to it.

Sera went through the kitchen into the sitting room, at the front of the house, still wearing her jacket.

I'm glad you're wearing that now, he said, especially with hunting season coming on.

She didn't speak to Pep and he made the mistake of following her back into the kitchen.

Why, Sera asked, are you suddenly worried about what I'm wearing?

He thought for a moment.

I'm not saying. . . .

You're not saying anything. Just like you had nothing to

say to that woman when you pulled the horse out of the mine. You had nothing to say.

The incident had been months ago. It took him several seconds to scroll back his memory. His thinking became more difficult the longer he watched her face changing, turning red. When she was upset her forehead scrunched up and made her large eyebrows look like two squirrels fighting over a nut. Then all at once her eyes would just crumble. On those rare occasions, Pep was usually so absorbed in watching Sera's face that he had to focus on her mouth to concentrate on what she was telling him.

What are you talking about? That woman?

You, Sera said, her voice breaking, you brought her husband out of that mine and you had nothing to say to her. It was a job for you. I saw that. I saw you. Everyone saw you just standing there. But I was waiting for them to come out, she finished. I was waiting.

Pep, open-mouthed, tried to stammer something as she turned and walked out of the room.

Sera was in bed when he caught up to her, five minutes later, with something to say. She'd rolled to the far edge, her back to him, leaving Pep most of the bed and almost none of the blankets. But she was further away than that.

She was asleep.

At least he hoped she was.

Pep turned off the light and undressed in the dark, slid onto the cold mattress. Her shoulder was just as cold when he brushed it. Pep pulled some of the blankets toward him, over her bare shoulder, and listened to the sound of her breath whispering against her forearm. For the first time he could remember, he looked at the ceiling without wondering if it needed painting or cleaning. He just breathed in the silence and let his eyes wander from corner to corner. Like mice.

Inside, as always, the tunnel is warm and humid. Water drips from the ceiling to the floor, measuring the darkness with splinks and splunks. One second drips, then dribbles into another. The minutes seep, trickle and collect into pools of hours: crude clocks that mark Celi's time inside the mountain. Strung together the drips create a steady pulse that veins through the dark, unseen. The sound becomes louder, overshadows his heart's rhythm. The pools grow, then dissipate and seep into other tunnels.

*

Every morning now, Pep straightened his little body up, out of the bed, and swung his legs down to the cold floor with a squeak that seemed to come more from his bones than the box springs. The first thing he did was light the Coleman stove with yesterday's newspaper and whatever kitchen scraps he'd left on the counters: a milk carton, sometimes an orange peel. He wore only a pair of urine-stained underwear and a long, loose undershirt that hung low, sagging like the skin on his kneecaps.

He moved back to the bedroom when the paper was lit and the kindling crackled. He shovelled coal into the stove later, with a small, flat hand shovel that sat in a coal scuttle. A four-by-four sheet of stainless steel kept the kitchen linoleum safe from the stove's heat and sparks.

As Pep reached for a weathered pair of pants from a side chair his biceps stretched, then knotted into tiny baseballs. He lowered his pants to the floor and carefully lifted one foot into a hole, pulled them up, then down, and stepped in with the other foot. His body was stiff in the morning. Even his lungs were slow to start. He hacked up some black phlegm—his miner's badge—from his throat but saved it until he got back to the stove. He had trouble getting his arms back and into his shirtsleeves, as if he were pushing up a heavy weight instead of pulling his shirt down. His hands moved more awkwardly the higher he raised them, trying to slide the shirt over his elbows.

He didn't eat breakfast until later, at the café, after he'd packed a lunch, put on his sweat-stained hat and dragged his shadow downtown.

Two weeks ago I had the best bowel movement in the country, he said to himself, or something like that. Pep looked stern, expecting his listener to challenge him, whether or not anyone was near him.

And now all of a sudden my whole insides have turned against me. Prune juice twice a day, then some roughage, not much mind you, just this bowl of bran flakes.

If he felt more talkative he gave someone a lecture on the perils of the day: you should see the stuff they're shoving into people these days. Antacids, preservatives, chemicals. Hey, I even heard you can make an oil lamp out of a McDonald's shake if you leave it alone for a week—that's your petrol chemicals for you. It's not like it was, let me tell you. The world's changed.

If he thought about Sera, he didn't reveal much.

Hey, she could cook. Meatballs *come stronzo*—just like horse shit: that doesn't quite translate into English very well but they say that in Italian, if your meatballs are really good. If they have that texture, you know. There's different words for everything, every kind of shit, but horse shit is particularly durable, has a woven compactness.

She knew how to do that just right. And she'd serve it all, with the spaghetti or linguine, on a warm plate. He remembered that she warmed the empty bowls in the stove, sort of like chilling a glass before you start pouring the wine. Jeez it made a difference. Grated the *parmigiana* over the dish so the flakes kind of drifted down over the food and didn't settle hard-like on top. You never tasted anything like it.

Probably, that was the most he said about her in a year. He was quiet for odd moments, reflective. His eyes opened and closed. Then he shrugged his shoulders, sipped the last of his coffee and got up from his table.

After digging in his pocket he left two-bits by the cup. He reached for his hat and made for the door, on his way to count tags at the mine.

TWELVE

What she sees:

 She listens for his breathing to become regular, measured by a deep inhalation, a cool nasal spray of air on the back of her neck and a long—remarkably long—moment of silence before each new breath. After half an hour Sera slips her hand out from under her pillow, pulls back her side of the blankets, quietly scissors her legs over the side of the bed and ends in a partial squat, eyes level with her husband's breathing, twitching face. Pep is sleeping soundly, his breathing regular, methodical. She can imagine him working in the mine with the same rhythm, his lungs keeping time with the pick in his hand as if he needs the coal face to breathe. The shadow that falls on his cheek makes a labyrinth of lines across his face, spread out from the corners of his eyes like the belly of a leaf. Sera reaches for her skirt and slippers. Instead of taking them out of the room to put on, she dresses in front of her husband's closed eyelids, tucking her flannel nightgown into her skirt and balancing herself with the back of a chair while she slips on one slipper, then the other. Then, she puts on her jacket, Pep's red hunting jacket, and, one resolute step after another, she walks out of his world.

*

Snow was falling. It illuminated the night.

 While the wind was lighter, having released most of its

tempest, there was still a fairly strong current that rushed the snow almost parallel with the ground. The snow whisked toward her face, then over her head like a white bird in the night. A snow owl.

Walking to the road, she closed her eyes to let the snowflakes hook, then hang from her lashes. Her strong ankles carved a path through whiteness. When she reached the street, feeling her slippers scratch, then clack against the pavement, she blinked her eyelashes free. She felt warm.

The moon was out, but behind the snow it was only a white smudge in a speckled sky, the snow like falling flakes of moon.

*

There is only one miner's tag missing. The men Pep sends would have missed him completely if one of the searchers hadn't wanted to check an older room, unused but still partially open. The roof hasn't caved properly behind the miners who left it. The room is buttressed with a forest of timbers that bow under the floor's pressure, pushing up the roof. Some of the timbers fortify what is left of the hollowed-out pillars, but the checkboards at the bottom of the room's chute are full of fallen slack and cap rock. The room is ready to fall.

And yet their lamps cleave into the room's darkness. They find Celi lying on his side, alone in a puddle beside one of those timbers. His eyes are closed. He's next to the coal face. Strong arms lift and carry Celi around his shoulders, more hands on his legs, under his knees. The light that bobs next to him against the walls barely punctures the dark. Another six hundred yards and they will be out. Doc Sunderd will check him over, even though the cause of death is apparent enough: blackdamp. The gas got to him. As they carry Celi down the slope toward the entrance, fingers of methane swirl past them. The gas currents spiral behind them. And the timbers rock and creak against the nuts, cobbles, peas and fines.

*

In the morning, when Pep woke, there was a blanket of snow on the road. The blanket stretched a whiteness two miles long, two hundred blankets long, partially covering Sera's footprints, the street and her path back to the mine.

The house shielded some of their yard from the night's flurries. Nearest the house there was no snow at all, so Sera's tracks began not at the door but in the middle of the lawn. Narrow slices, like empty parentheses, slashed smoothly through the snow. Her footprints disappeared under the blanket and only the parentheses remained.

Etched in whiteness, they blurred easily.

As Pep dressed for work, the snow blew right into the mine entrance and lit up the mouth of the tunnel like a salt mine or a fairy cavern. The tunnel's entrance changed from white to black as quickly as sugar vanished into his coffee. The temperature changed just as remarkably.

The wind was behind her.

And on a hook, just inside the mine—between day and night—she left Pep's jacket.

*

Serafina slips into the darkness, sinking into its world without a sound. Her eyes close—there is no difference from when they are open—and she sleeps. Long ropes of methane marble the darkness. The mine's current twists and swirls all around her. It gently tugs and pulls her night's thoughts through the tunnel, through the mountain. There are moments of silence (the only thing that splinters such heavy darkness), then the sounds of footsteps clacking rhythmically against the floor and distant waves crashing against distant walls. She hears the ropes tightening, pulling row-boats that creak their way through tunnels. And her sleep, coloured with dreams, draws her home.

***

Acknowledgements

A number of books were important to me in my research: *The Crowsnest and Its People*, written by the people themselves and assembled by the Crowsnest Pass Historical Society, 1979. Frank Anderson and Elsie Turnbull's *Tragedies of the Crowsnest Pass*, 1983. John Robert Colombo's *Mysterious Canada*, 1988. William J. Robinson's *Sexual Problems of Today*, 1921. *Useful Household Helps, Hints and Recipes* published in 1916 by Theo Audel. *Customs and Habits of the Sicilian Peasants*, written by Salvatore Salomone-Marino in 1897, edited and translated by Rosalie N. Norris, 1981. And Henry Swinburne's *Travels in the Two Sicilies*, Edizioni Parallelo, 1976.

Special thanks go to the A.T.J. Cairns Memorial Foundation and the Department of English at the University of Calgary. To the Crowsnest Pass Historical Society and the Coleman Museum, for letting me look into their archives, mining photographs and safety lamps. And finally, to Signora Foti Mazzone, for her faith and her friendship.

PRINTED IN CANADA